# THE PIRATES
# OF ZAN

# THE PIRATES OF ZAN

## MURRAY LEINSTER

**WILDSIDE PRESS**

# CHAPTER I

It had not been impulsive action when Bron Hoddan had started for the planet Walden by stowing away on a police ship that had come to his native planet to hang all his relatives. He'd planned it long before. Getting to Walden had been his long-cherished dream. As it had turned out, his relatives had not been hanged. This they had avoided with their usual technique of acting aggrieved and innocent. They had given proof that they were simple people leading blameless lives. They had made their would-be executioners feel ashamed and apologetic. And, as soon as the strangers had left, Bron knew that these "simple, blameless" folk had returned to their normal way of life, which was piracy.

Bron's stow-away ride had only taken him partway to Walden. It had taken him a long time to earn the rest of his passage, since he had to travel from one solar system to another. But he had held to his idea. Walden was the most civilized planet in that part of the galaxy. On Walden Bron had intended, (a) to achieve splendid things as an electronic engineer, (b) to grow satisfyingly rich, (c) to marry a delightful girl, and (d) end his life with the reputation of being a great man.

He had spent his first two years on Walden trying to achieve the first of his objectives.

And it was only the night before the police broke into his room, that the accomplishment of his first objective seemed imminent.

He had gone to bed and slept soundly. He was calmly sure that his ambitions were about to be realized. At practically any instant his brilliance would be discovered and he'd be well-to-do; his friend Derec would admire him, and even Nedda would probably decide to marry him right away.

Bron was happy to be on Walden, it was a fine world. Outside the capital city was the spaceport that received shipments of luxuries and raw materials from halfway across the galaxy. Its landing-grid reared skyward and tapped the planet's ionosphere for power with which to hoist ships to clear-space and pluck down others from emptiness. There was commerce and manufacturing, wealth and culture, and Walden modestly admitted that its standard of living was the highest in the Nurmi cluster. Its citizens had no reason to worry about anything but a supply of tranquilizers to enable them to stand the boredom of their lives.

Even Hoddan was satisfied, as of the moment. On his native planet there wasn't even a landing-grid. The few battered ships the inhabitants owned had to take off precariously on rockets. They came back blackened and more battered and sometimes they were accompanied by great hulls whose crews and passengers were mysteriously missing. These extra ships had to be landed on their emergency rockets, and of course couldn't take off again, but they always vanished quickly just the same. And the people of Zan, on which Hoddan had been born, always affected innocent indignation when embattled spacecraft came and furiously demanded that they be produced.

There were some people who said that all the inhabitants of Zan were space-pirates and ought to be hanged; compared with such a planet, Walden seemed a very fine place indeed. So on a certain night Bron Hoddan went confidently to bed and slept soundly until three hours after sunrise. Then the police broke in his door.

They made a tremendous crash in doing it, but they were in great haste. The noise waked Hoddan, and he blinked his eyes open. Before he could stir, four uniformed men grabbed him and dragged him out of bed. They searched him frantically for anything like a weapon. Then they stood him against a wall with two stun-pistols on him, and the main body of cops began to tear his room apart. He could not guess what they were looking for. Then his friend Derec came hesitantly to the door and looked at him remorsefully. He wrung his hands.

"I had to do it, Bron," he said agitatedly. "I couldn't help doing it!"

"What's happened?" asked Hoddan blankly. "What's this about?"

Derec said miserably:

"You killed someone, Bron. An innocent man! You didn't mean to, but you did…it's terrible!"

"*Me*, kill somebody! That's ridiculous!" protested Hoddan.

"They found him outside the power-house," said Derec bitterly. "Outside the Mid-Continent station that you—"

"Mid-Continent? Oh!" Hoddan was relieved. It was amazing how much he was relieved. He'd had a terrible fear for a moment that somebody might have found out he'd been born and raised on Zan. This would have ruined everything. It was almost impossible to imagine, but still it was a great relief to find out he was only suspected of a murder he hadn't committed. And he was only suspected because his first great achievement as an electronic engineer had been discovered. "They found the thing at Mid-Continent, eh? But I didn't kill anybody. And there's no harm done. The thing's been running two weeks, now. I was going to the Power Board in a couple of days." He addressed the police. "I know what's up, now," he said. "Give me some clothes and let's go get this straightened out."

A cop waved a stun-pistol at him.

"One word out of line, and it's pfft!"

"Don't talk, Bron!" said Derec in panic. "Just keep quiet! It's bad enough! Don't make it worse."

A cop handed Hoddan a garment. He put it on. He became aware that the cop was scared. So was Derec. Everybody in the room was scared except himself. Hoddan found himself incredulous. People didn't act this way on super-civilized, highest-peak-of-culture Walden.

"Who'd I kill?" he demanded. "And why?"

"You wouldn't know him, Bron," said Derec mournfully. "You didn't mean to do murder. But it's only luck that you killed only him instead of everybody."

"*Everybody*!" Hoddan stared.

"No more talk!" snapped the nearest cop. His teeth were chattering. "Keep quiet or else!"

Hoddan shut up. His clothing was inspected and then handed to him. He dressed while the cops completed the examination of his room. They were insanely thorough, though Hoddan hadn't the least idea what they might be looking for. When they began to rip up the floor and pull down the walls, the other cops led him outside.

There was a fleet of police trucks in the shaded street. They piled him in one, and four cops climbed after him, keeping stun-pistols trained on him during the maneuver. Out of the corner of his eye he saw Derec climbing into another truck. The entire fleet sped away. The whole affair had been taken with enormous seriousness by the police. Traffic was detoured from their route. When they swung up on an elevated expressway, there was no other vehicle in sight. They raced on downtown.

They rolled off the expressway, then down a cleared avenue. Hoddan recognized the Detention Building. Its gate swung wide. The truck he rode in went inside. The gate closed. The other trucks went away, rapidly. Hoddan alighted and saw that the grim, gray wall of the courtyard had a surprising number of guards mustered to sweep the open space with gunfire if anybody made a suspicious movement.

He shook his head. Nobody had mentioned Zan, so this simply didn't make sense. His conscience was wholly clear except about his native planet. This was insanity! He went curiously into the building and into the hearing-room. His guards surrendered him to courtroom guards and went away with almost hysterical haste. Nobody wanted to be near him.

Hoddan stared about. The courtroom was highly informal. The justice sat at an ordinary desk. There were comfortable chairs. The air was clean. The atmosphere was that of a conference room in which reasonable men could discuss differences of opinion in calm leisure. Only on a world like Walden would a police prisoner be dealt with in such surroundings.

Derec came in by another door, with him a man Hoddan recognized as the attorney who'd represented Nedda's father in certain past interviews. There'd been no mention of Nedda at these meetings; it had been strictly business. Nedda's father was chairman of the Power Board, a director of the Planetary Association of Manufacturers, a committeeman of the Bankers' League, and he held other important posts. Hoddan had been thrown out of his offices several times. He now scowled ungraciously at the lawyer who had ordered him thrown out. He saw Derec wringing his hands.

An agitated man in court uniform came to his side.

"I'm the citizen's representative," he said uneasily. "I'm to look after your interests. Do you want a personal lawyer?"

"Why?" asked Hoddan. He felt splendidly confident.

"The charges... Do you wish a psychiatric examination, claiming no responsibility?" asked the representative anxiously. "It might—it might really be best."

"I'm not crazy," said Hoddan.

The citizen's representative spoke to the justice.

"Sir, the accused waives psychiatric examination, without prejudice to a later claim of no responsibility."

Nedda's father's attorney watched with bland eyes. Hoddan said impatiently:

"Let's get started so this will make some sense! I know what I've done. Now, what monstrous crime am I charged with?"

"The charges against you," said the justice politely, "are that on the night of three, twenty-seven last, you, Bron Hoddan, entered the fenced-in grounds surrounding the Mid-Continent power receptor station. It is charged that you passed two no-admittance signs. You arrived at a door marked 'Authorized Personnel Only.' You broke the lock of that door. Inside, you smashed the power receptor. This power receptor converts broadcast power for industrial units by which two hundred thousand men are employed. You smashed the receptor, imperiling their employment." The justice paused. "Do you wish to challenge any of these charges as contrary to fact?"

The citizen's representative said hurriedly:

"You have the right to deny any of them, of course."

"Why should I?" asked Hoddan. "I did them! But what's this about my killing somebody? Why'd they tear my place apart looking for something? Who'd I kill, anyhow?"

"Don't bring that up!" pleaded the citizen's representative. "Please don't bring that up! You will be much, much better off if that is not mentioned!"

"But I didn't kill anybody!" insisted Hoddan.

"Nobody's said a word about it," said the citizen's representative, jittering. "Let's not have it in the record! The record has to be published!" He turned to the justice. "Sir, the facts are conceded as stated."

"Then," said the justice to Hoddan, "do you choose to answer these charges at this time?"

"Why not?" asked Hoddan. "Of course!"

"Proceed," said the justice.

Hoddan drew a deep breath. He didn't understand why the man's death, charged to him, was not mentioned. He didn't like the scared way everybody looked at him.

"About the burglary business," he said confidently. "What did I do in the power station before I smashed the receptor?"

The justice looked at Nedda's father's attorney.

"Why," said that gentleman amiably," speaking for the Power Board as complainant, before you smashed the standard receptor you connected a device of your own design across the power leads. It was a receptor unit of an apparently original pattern. It appears to have been a very interesting device."

"I'd offered it to the Power Board," said Hoddan, with satisfaction, "and I was thrown out. You had me thrown out! What did it do?"

"It substituted for the receptor you smashed," said the attorney. "It continued to supply some two hundred million kilowatts for the Mid-Continent industrial area. In fact, your crime was only discovered because the original receptor had to be regularly serviced. Being set to draw peak power at all times, the unused power is wasted by burning carbon. Your device adjusted to the load and did not burn carbon. So when the attendants went to replace the supposedly burned carbon and found it unused, they discovered what you had done."

"My receptor saved carbon, then," said Hoddan triumphantly. "That means it saved money. I saved the Power Board plenty while it was connected! They wouldn't believe I could. Now they know. I did!"

The justice said:

"Irrelevant. You have the charges. In legal terms, you are charged with burglary, trespassing, breaking and entering, unlawful entry, malicious mischief, breach of the peace, sabotage, and endangering the employment of citizens. Discuss the charges, please!"

"I'm telling you!" protested Hoddan. "I offered the thing to the Power Board. They said they were satisfied with what they had and wouldn't listen. So I proved what they wouldn't listen to! That receptor saved them ten thousand credits' worth of carbon a week! It'll save half a million credits a year in every power station that uses it! If I know the Power Board, they're going right on using it while they arrest me for putting it to work!"

The courtroom, in its entirety, visibly shivered.

"Aren't they?" demanded Hoddan belligerently.

"They are not," said the justice, tight-lipped. "It has been smashed and melted down."

"Then they'll look at my patents!" insisted Hoddan. "It's stupid—"

"The patent records," said the justice with unnecessary vehemence, "have been destroyed. Your possessions have been searched for copies. Nobody will ever look at your drawings again—not if they are wise!"

"Wha-a-at?" demanded Hoddan incredulously. "Wha-a-at?"

"I will amend the record of this hearing before it is published," said the justice shakily. "I should not have made that comment. I ask permission of the citizen's representative to amend."

"Granted," said the representative before he had finished. The justice said quickly:

"The charges have been admitted by the defendant. Since the complainant does not wish punitive action taken against him—"

"He'd be silly if he did," grunted Hoddan.

"—and merely wishes security against repetition of the offense, I rule that the defendant may be released upon posting suitable bond for good behavior in the future. That is, he will be required to post bond which will be forfeited if he ever again enters a power station enclosure, passes no-trespassing signs, ignores no-admittance signs, and/or smashes apparatus belonging to the complainant."

"All right," said Hoddan indignantly. "I'll raise it somehow. If they're too stupid to save money... How much bond?"

"The court will take it under advisement and will notify the defendant within the customary two hours," said the justice at top speed. He swallowed. "The defendant will be kept in close confinement until the bond is posted. The hearing is ended."

He did not look at Hoddan. Courtroom guards put stun-pistols against Hoddan's body and ushered him out.

Presently his friend Derec came to see him in the tool-steel cell in which he had been placed. Derec looked white and stricken.

"I'm in trouble because I'm your friend, Bron," he said miserably, "but I asked permission to explain things to you. After all, I caused your arrest. I urged you not to connect up your receptor without permission!"

"I know," growled Hoddan, "but there are some people so stupid you have to show them everything. I didn't realize that there are people so stupid you can't show them anything!"

"You showed something you didn't intend," said Derec miserably. "Bron, I—I have to tell you. When they went to charge the carbon bins at the power station, they—they found a dead man, Bron!"

Hoddan sat up.

"What's that?"

"Your machine...killed him. He was outside the building at the foot of a tree. Your receptor killed him through a stone wall! It broke his bones and killed him." Derec wrung his hands. "At some stage of power-drain your receptor makes death rays!"

Hoddan had had a good many shocks today. When Derec arrived, he'd been incredulously comparing the treatment he'd received and the panic about him, with the charges made against him in court. They didn't add up. This new, previously undisclosed item left him speechless. He goggled at Derec, who fairly wept.

"Don't you see?" asked Derec pleadingly. "That's why I had to tell the police it was you. We can't have death rays! The police can't let anybody go free who knows how to make them! This is a wonderful world, but there are lots of crackpots. They'll do anything! The police daren't let it even be suspected that death rays can be made! That's why you weren't charged with murder. People all over the planet would start doing research, and sooner or later would come up with what you discovered. With such a tool in the hands of the crackpots, life would be cheap, indeed! For the sake of our civilization your secret has to be suppressed—and you with it. It's terrible for you, Bron, but there's nothing else to do!"

Hoddan said dazedly:

"But I only have to put up a bond to be released!"

"The justice," said Derec tearfully, "didn't name it in court, because it would have to be published. But he's set your bond at fifty million credits! Nobody could raise that for you, Bron! And with the reason for it what it is, you'll never be able to get it reduced!"

"But anybody who looks at the plans of the receptor will know it can't make death rays!" protested Hoddan blankly.

"Nobody will look," said Derec tearfully. "Anybody who knows how to make it will have to be locked up. They checked the patent examiners. They've forgotten. Nobody dared examine the device you had working. They'd be jailed if they understood it! Nobody will ever risk learning how to make death rays—not on a world as civilized as this, with so many people anxious to kill everybody else. You have to be locked up forever, Bron. You have to!"

Hoddan said inadequately:

"Oh."

"I beg your forgiveness for having you arrested," said Derec in abysmal sorrow, "but I couldn't do anything but tell…"

Hoddan stared at his cell wall. Derec went away weeping. He was an admirable, honorable, not-too-bright young man who had been Hoddan's only friend.

Hoddan stared blankly at nothing. As an event, it was preposterous, and yet it was wholly natural. When in the course of human events somebody does something that puts somebody else to the trouble of adjusting the numb routine of his life, the adjustee is resentful. The richer he is and the more satisfactory he considers his life, the more resentful he is at any change, however minute. And of all the changes which offend people, changes which require them to think are most disliked. The high brass on the Power Board considered that everything was moving smoothly. There was no need to consider new devices. Hoddan's drawings and plans had simply never been bothered with, because there was no recognized need for them. And when he forced acknowledgement that his receptor worked, the unwelcome demonstration was highly offensive in itself. It was natural, it was inevitable, it should have been infallibly certain that any possible excuse for not thinking about the receptor would be seized upon. And a single dead man found near the operating demonstrator… Now, if one assumed that the demonstrator had killed him, why one could react emotionally, feel vast indignation, frantically command that the device and its inventor be suppressed together—and then go on living happily without doing any thinking or making any other change in anything at all.

Hoddan was appalled. Now that it had happened, he could see that it had to. The world of Walden was at the very peak of human culture. It had arrived at so splendid a plane of civilization that nobody could imagine any improvement; unless a better tranquilizer could be designed to make the boredom more endurable. Nobody can want anything he doesn't know exists, or that he can't imagine to exist. On Walden nobody wanted anything, unless it was relief from the tedium of ultra-civilized life. Hoddan's electronic device did not fill a human need only a technical one. It had therefore, no value that would make anybody hospitable to it.

And Hoddan would spend his life in jail for failing to recognize this fact soon enough.

He revolted immediately. *He* wanted something! He wanted out. He set about designing his escape. He put his mind to work on the problem, simply and directly. And this time he would not make the mistake of furnishing other people with what they did not want. He took the view that he must *seem,* at least, to give his captors and jailers and—as he saw it—his persecutors, what they wanted.

They would be pleased to have him dead, provided their consciences were clear. He built on that as a foundation.

Very shortly before nightfall he performed certain cryptic actions. He unraveled threads from his shirt and put them aside. There would be a vision-lens in the ceiling of his cell, and somebody would certainly notice what he did. He turned on a light. He put the threads in his mouth, set fire to his mattress, and lay down calmly upon it. The mattress was of excellent quality. It would smell very badly as it smoldered.

It did. Lying flat, he kicked convulsively for a few seconds. He looked like somebody who had taken poison. Then he waited.

It was a long time before his jailer came down the corridor, dragging a fire hose. Hoddan had been correct in assuming that he was watched. His actions had been those of a man who'd anticipated a possible need to commit suicide, and who'd had poison in a part of his shirt for convenience. The jailer did not hurry, because if the inventor of a death ray committed suicide, everybody would feel better. Hoddan had been allowed a reasonable time in which to die.

He seemed impressively dead when the jailer opened his cell door, dragged him out, removed the so-far-unscorched other furniture, and set up the fire hose to make an aerosol fog which would put out the fire. He went back to the corridor to wait for the fire to be extinguished.

Hoddan crowned him with a stool, feeling an unexpected satisfaction in the act. The jailer collapsed.

He did not carry keys. The system was for him to be let out of this corridor by a guard outside. Hoddan took the fire hose. He turned its nozzle back to make a stream instead of a mist. Water came out at four hundred pounds pressure. He smashed open the corridor door with it. He strolled through and bowled over a startled guard with the same stream. He took the guard's stun-pistol. He washed open another door leading to the courtyard. He marched out, washed down two guards who sighted him, and took the trouble to flush them across the pavement until they wedged in a drain opening. Then he thoughtfully reset the hose to fill the courtyard with fog, climbed into the driver's seat of a parked truck, started it, and smashed through the gateway to the street outside. Behind him, the courtyard filled with dense white mist.

He was free, but only temporarily. Around him lay the capital city of Walden—the highest civilization in this part of the galaxy. Trees lined its ways. Towers rose splendidly toward the skies, with thousands of less ambitious structures in between. There were open squares and parkways and malls, and it did not smell like a city at all. But he wasn't loose three minutes before the communicator in the truck squawked the all-police alarm for him.

It was to be expected. All the city would shortly be one enormous man trap, set to catch Bron Hoddan. There was only one place on the planet, in fact, where he could be safe. And ironically, he wouldn't have been safe there if he'd been officially charged with murder. But since the police had tactfully failed to mention murder, he could get at least breathing-time by taking refuge in the Interstellar Embassy.

He headed for it, bowling along splendidly. The police truck hummed on its way until the great open square before the embassy became visible. The embassy was not that of a single planet, of course. By pure necessity every human-inhabited world was independent of all others, but the Interstellar Diplomatic Service represented humanity at large upon each individual globe. Its ambassador was the only person who Hoddan could even imagine as listening to him, and that because he came from off-planet, as Hoddan did. But he mainly counted upon a breathing-space in the embassy, during which to make more plans as yet unformed and unformable. He began, though, to see some virtues in the simple, lawless, piratical world on which he had spent his childhood.

Another police truck rushed frantically toward him down a side street. Stun-pistols made little pinging noises against the body of his vehicle. He put on more speed, but the other truck overtook him. It ranged alongside, its occupants bellowing stern commands to halt. And then, just before they swerved to force him off the highway, he swung instead and they crashed thunderously. One of his own wheels collapsed. He drove on with the crumpled wheel producing an up-and-down motion that threatened to make him seasick. Then he heard yelling behind him. The cops had piled out of the truck and were in pursuit on foot.

The, tall, stone wall of the embassy was visible, now, beyond the monument to the first settlers of Walden. He leaped to the ground and ran. Stun-pistol bolts, a little beyond their effective range, stung like fire. They spurred him on.

The gate of the embassy was closed. He bolted around the corner and scrambled up the conveniently rugged stones of the wall. He was well aloft before the cops spotted him. Then they fired at him industriously and the charges crackled all around him.

But he'd reached the top and had both arms over the parapet before a charge hit his legs and paralyzed them. He hung fast, swearing at his bad luck.

Then hands grasped his wrists. A white-haired man appeared on the other side of the parapet. He took a good, solid grip, and heaved. He drew Hoddan over the top of the wall and helped him down to the walkway.

"A near thing, that!" said the white-haired man pleasantly. "I was taking a walk in the garden when I heard the excitement. I got to the wall just in time." He paused, and added, "I do hope you're not just a common murderer, we can't offer asylum to such. But if you're a political offender…"

Hoddan began to try to rub sensation and usefulness back into his legs. Feeling came back, and was not pleasant.

"I'm the Interstellar Ambassador," said the white-haired man politely.

"My name," said Hoddan bitterly," is Bron Hoddan and I'm guilty of trying to save the Power Board millions of credits a year!" Then he said more bitterly, "If you want to know, I ran away from Zan to try to be a civilized man and live a civilized life. It was a mistake! Now I'm to be permanently jailed for using my brains!"

The ambassador cocked his head thoughtfully to one side.

"Zan?" he said. "The name Hoddan fits with that somehow… Oh, yes! Space-piracy! They say the people of Zan capture and loot a dozen or so ships a year, only there's no way to prove it on them. And there's a man named Hoddan who's supposed to head a particularly ruffianly gang."

"My grandfather," said Hoddan defiantly. "What are you going to do about it? I'm outlawed! I've defied the planetary government! I'm disreputable by descent, and worst of all I've tried to use my brains!"

"Deplorable!" said the ambassador mildly. "I don't mean outlawry is deplorable, you understand, or defiance of the government, or being disreputable. But trying to use one's brains is bad business! A serious offense! Are your legs all right now? Then come on down with me and I'll have you given some dinner and some fresh clothing. Offhand," he added amiably, "it would seem that using one's brains would be classed as a political offense rather than a criminal one on Walden. We'll see."

Hoddan gaped up at him.

"You mean there's a possibility that—"

"Of course!" said the ambassador in surprise. "You haven't phrased it that way, but you're actually a rebel. A revolutionist. You defy authority and tradition and governments and such things. Naturally the Interstellar Diplomatic Service is inclined to be on your side! What do you think it's for?"

# CHAPTER II

In something under two hours Hoddan was ushered into the ambassador's office. He'd been refreshed, his torn clothing replaced by more respectable garments, and the places where stun-pistols had stung him, soothed by ointments. But, more important, he'd worked out and firmly adopted a new point of view.

He'd been a misfit at home on Zan. He was not contented with the humdrum and monotonous life as a member of a space-pirate community. Piracy was a matter of dangerous take-offs in cranky rocket ships, to be followed by weeks or months of tedious and uncomfortable boredom in highly unhealthy re-breathed air. No voyage ever contained more than ten seconds of satisfactory action. All fighting took place just out of the atmosphere of the embattled planet. Regardless of the result of the fight, the pirates had to get away fast when it was over, lest overwhelming forces swarm up from the nearby world. It was intolerably devoid of anything an ambitious young man would want.

Even when one had made a good prize—with the lifeboats of the foreign ship darting frantically for ground—and even after one got back to Zan with the captured ship, even then there was little satisfaction to a pirate's career. Zan had not a large population. Piracy couldn't support a large number of people. Zan couldn't attempt to defend itself against even single, heavily armed ships that sometimes came in passionate resolve to avenge the disappearance of a rich freighter or a fast, new liner. So the people of Zan, to avoid being hanged, had to play innocent. They had to be convincingly simple, harmless folk who cultivated their fields and lived quiet, blameless lives. They might loot, but they couldn't use their loot where investigators could find it. They had to build their own houses and make their own furniture and grow their own food. So life on Zan was dull. Piracy was not profitable in the sense that one could live well by it. It simply wasn't a trade for anybody like Hoddan.

So he'd abandoned all that. He'd studied electronics in books looted from passenger-ship libraries. Within months after his arrival on a law-abiding planet, he was able to earn a living at electronics as an honest trade.

And that was unsatisfactory, too. Law-abiding communities were no more thrilling or rewarding than piratical ones. A pay-day now and then did not make up for the tedium of earning. Even when one had money there was not much to do with it. On Walden, to be sure, the level of civilization was so high that most people took to psychiatric treatments so they could stand it, and the neurotics vastly outnumbered the more normal folk. But on Walden, electronics was only a way to make a living, like piracy, and there was no more fun to be had out of being civilized.

What Hoddan craved, of course, was a sense of achievement. Technically, there were opportunities all about him. He'd developed one, and it would save millions of credits a year if it were adopted. But it did not happen to be anything that anybody wanted. He'd tried to force its use and he was in trouble. Now he saw clearly that a law-abiding world was no more satisfactory than a piratical one.

The ambassador received him with a cordial wave of the hand.

"Things move fast," he said cheerfully. "You weren't here half an hour before there was a police captain at the gate. He explained that an excessively dangerous criminal had escaped jail and been seen climbing the embassy wall. He very generously offered to bring some men in and capture you and take you away—with my permission, of course. He was shocked when I declined."

"I can understand that," said Hoddan.

"By the way," said the ambassador. "Young men like yourself… Ah…is there a girl involved in this?"

Hoddan considered.

"A girl's father," he acknowledged, "is the real complainant against me."

"Does he complain," asked the ambassador, "because you want to marry her, or because you don't?"

"Neither," Hoddan told him. "She hasn't quite decided that I'm worth defying her rich father for."

"Good!" said the ambassador. "It can't be too bad a mess while a woman is being really practical. I've checked your story. Allowing for differences of viewpoint, it agrees with the official version. I've ruled that you are a political refugee, and so entitled to sanctuary in the embassy. And that's that."

"Thank you, sir," said Hoddan.

"There's no question about the crime," observed the ambassador, "or that it is primarily political. You proposed to improve a technical process in a society which considers itself beyond improvement. If you'd succeeded, the idea of change would have spread, people now poor would have gotten rich, people now rich would have gotten poor, and you'd have done what all governments are established to prevent. So you'll never be able to walk the streets of this planet again in safety. You've scared people."

"Yes, sir," said Hoddan. It's been an unpleasant surprise to them, to be scared."

The ambassador put the tips of his fingers together.

"Do you realize," he asked, "that the whole purpose of civilization is to take the surprises out of life, so one can be bored to death? That a culture in which nothing unexpected ever happens is in what is called its 'golden age?' That when nobody can even imagine anything happening unexpectedly, that they later fondly refer to that period as the 'good old days?'"

"I hadn't thought of it in just those words, sir."

"It is one of the most-avoided facts of life," said the ambassador. "Government, in the local or planetary sense of the word, is an organization for the suppression of adventure. Taxes are, in part, the insurance premiums one pays for protection against the unpredictable. And your act has been an offense against everything that is the foundation of a stable, orderly and damnably tedious way of life—against civilization, in fact."

Hoddan frowned.

"Yet, you've granted me asylum."

"Naturally!" said the ambassador. "The Diplomatic Service works for the welfare of humanity. That doesn't mean stuffiness. A golden age in any civilization is always followed by collapse.

In ancient days savages came and camped outside the walls of super-civilized towns. They were unwashed, unmannerly, and unsanitary. Super-civilized people refused even to think about them! So presently the savages stormed the city walls and another civilization went up in flames."

"But now," objected Hoddan, "there are no savages."

"They invent themselves," the ambassador told him. "My point is that the Diplomatic Service cherishes individuals and causes which battle stuffiness and complacency and golden ages and monstrous things like that. Not thieves, of course. They're degradation, like body-lice. But rebels and crackpots and revolutionaries who prevent hardening of the arteries of commerce and furnish wholesome exercise to the body politic—they're worth cherishing!"

"I think I see, sir," said Hoddan.

"I hope you do," said the ambassador. "My action on your behalf is pure diplomatic policy. To encourage the dissatisfied is to insure against the menace of universal satisfaction. Walden is in a bad way. You are the most encouraging thing that has happened here in a long time. And you're not a native."

"No-o-o," agreed Hoddan. "I come from Zan."

"Never mind." The ambassador turned to a stellar atlas. "Consider yourself a good symptom, and valued as such. If you could start a contagion, you'd be doing a service to your fellow citizens. Savages can always invent themselves. But enough…let us set about your affairs." He consulted the atlas. "Where would you like to go, since you must leave Walden?"

"Not too far, sir."

"The girl, eh?" The ambassador did not smile. He ran his finger down a page. "The nearest inhabited worlds are Krim and Darth. Krim is a place of lively commercial activity, where an electronics engineer should easily find employment. It is said to be progressive and there is much organized research."

"I wouldn't want to be a kept engineer, sir," said Hoddan apologetically. "I'd rather—well—putter on my own."

"Impractical, but sensible," commented the ambassador. He turned a page. "There's Darth. Its social system is practically feudal. It's technically backward. There's a landing-grid, but space-exports are skins and metal ingots and practically nothing else. There is no broadcast power. Strangers find the local customs difficult. There is no town larger than twenty thousand people, and few approach that size. Most settled places are mere villages near some feudal castle, and roads are so few and bad that wheeled transport is rare."

He leaned back and said in a detached voice:

"I had a letter from there a couple of months ago. It was rather arrogant. The writer was one Don Loris, and he explained that his dignity would not let him make a commercial offer, but an electronic engineer who put himself under his protection would not be the loser. Are you interested? No kings on Darth, just feudal chiefs."

Hoddan thought it over.

"I'll go to Darth," he decided. "It's bound to be better than Zan, and it can't be worse than Walden."

The ambassador looked impassive. An embassy servant came in and offered an indoor communicator. The ambassador put it to his ear. After a moment he said:

"Show him in." He turned to Hoddan. "You did kick up a storm! The Minister of State, no less, is here to demand your surrender. I'll counter with a formal request for an exit permit. I'll talk to you again when he leaves."

Hoddan went out. He paced up and down the other room into which he was shown. Darth wouldn't be in a golden age! He was wiser now than he'd been just this morning He recognized that he'd made mistakes. Now he could see rather ruefully how completely improbable it was that anybody could put across a technical device merely by proving its value, without first making anybody want it. He shook his head regretfully at the blunder.

The ambassador sent for him.

"I've had a pleasant time," he told Hoddan genially. "There was a beautiful row. You've really scared people, Hoddan. You deserve well of the republic. Every government and every person needs to be thoroughly terrified occasionally. It limbers up the brain."

"Yes, sir," said Hoddan. "I've—"

"The planetary government," said the ambassador with relish, "insists that you have to be locked up with the key thrown away. It seems you know how to make death rays. I said it was nonsense, and you were a political refugee in sanctuary. The Minister of State said the Cabinet would consider removing you forcibly from the embassy if you weren't surrendered. I said that if the embassy were violated, no ship would clear for Walden from any other civilized planet. They wouldn't like losing their off-planet trade! Then he said that the government would not give you an exit permit, and that he would hold me personally responsible if you killed everybody on Walden, including himself and me. I said he insulted me by suggesting that I'd permit such shenanigans. He said the government would take an extremely grave view of my attitude, and I said they would be silly if they did. Then he went off with great dignity—but shaking with panic—to think up more nonsense."

"Evidently," said Hoddan in relief, "you believe me when I say that my gadget doesn't make death rays."

The ambassador looked slightly embarrassed.

"To be honest," he admitted, "I've no doubt that you invented it independently, but they've been using such a device for half a century in the Cetis cluster. They've had no trouble."

Hoddan winced.

"Did you tell the minister that?"

"Hardly," said the ambassador. "It would have done you no good. You're in open revolt and have performed overt acts of violence against the police. It was impolite enough for me to suggest that the local government was stupid. It would have been most undiplomatic to prove it."

Hoddan did not feel very proud, just then.

"I'm thinking that the cops—quite unofficially—might try to kidnap me from the embassy. They'll deny that they tried, especially if they manage it. But I think they'll try."

"Very likely," said the ambassador. "We'll take precautions."

"I'd like to make something—not lethal—just in case," said Hoddan. "If you can trust me not to make death rays, I'd like to make a generator of odd-shaped microwaves. They're described in textbooks. They ionize the air where they strike. That's all.

They make air a high-resistance conductor. Nothing more than that."

The ambassador said:

"There was an old-fashioned way to make ozone…" When Hoddan nodded, a little surprised, the ambassador said, "By all means go ahead! You should be able to get parts from your room vision-receiver. I'll have some tools given you." Then he added, Diplomacy has to understand the things that control events. Once it was social position. For a time it was weapons. Then it was commerce. Now it's technology. But I wonder how you'll use the ionization of air to protect yourself from kidnapers! Don't tell me! I'd rather try to guess."

He waved his hand in cordial dismissal and an embassy servant showed Hoddan to his quarters. Ten minutes later another staff man brought him tools. He was left alone.

He delicately disassembled the set in his room and began to put some of the parts together in a novel but wholly rational fashion. The science of electronics, like the science of mathematics, had progressed away beyond the point where all of it had practical application. One could spend a lifetime learning things that research had discovered in the past, and industry had never found a use for. On Zan, industriously reading pirated books, Hoddan hadn't known where utility stopped. He'd kept on learning long after a practical man would have stopped studying to get a paying job.

Any electronic engineer could have made the device he now assembled. It only needed to be wanted, and apparently he was the first person to want it. In this respect it was like the receptor that had gotten him into trouble. As he put the small parts together, he felt a certain loneliness. A man Hoddan's age needed to have some girl admire him from time to time. If Nedda had been sitting cross-legged before him, listening raptly while he explained, Hoddan would probably have been perfectly happy. But she wasn't. It wasn't likely she ever would be. Hoddan scowled.

Inside of an hour he'd made a hand-sized, five watt, guide projector of waves of eccentric form. In the beam of that projector, air became ionized. Air became a high-resistance conductor comparable to nichrome wire, when and where the projector sent its microwaves.

He was wrapping tape about the pistol-like hand-grip when a servant brought him a scribbled note. It had been handed in at the embassy gate by a woman who fled after leaving it. It looked like Nedda's handwriting. It read like Nedda's phrasing. It appeared to have been written by somebody in a highly emotional state. But it wasn't quite—not absolutely—convincing.

He went to find the ambassador. He handed over the note. The ambassador read it and raised his eyebrows.

"Well?"

"It could be authentic," admitted Hoddan.

"In other words," said the ambassador, "you are not sure that it is a booby trap—an invitation to a date with the police?"

"I'm not sure," said Hoddan. "I think I'd better bite. If I have any illusions left after this morning, I'd better find it out. I thought Nedda liked me quite a bit."

"I make no comment," observed the ambassador. "Can I help you in any way?"

"I have to leave the embassy," said Hoddan, "and there's almost a solid line of police outside the walls. Could I borrow some old clothes, a few pillows, and a length of rope?"

Half an hour later a rope uncoiled itself at the very darkest outside corner of the embassy wall. It dangled down to the ground. This was at the rear of the embassy enclosure. The night was bright with stars, and the city's towers glittered with many lights. But here there was almost complete blackness and that silence of a city which is sometimes so companionable.

The rope remained hanging from the wall. No light reached the ground there. The tiny crescent of Walden's farthest moon cast an insufficient glow. Nothing could be seen by it.

The rope went up, as if it had been lowered merely to make sure that it was long enough for its purpose. Then it descended again. This time a figure dangled at its end. It came down, swaying a little. It reached the blackest part of the shadow at the wall's base. It stayed there.

Nothing happened. The figure rose swiftly, hauled up in rapid pullings of the rope. Then the line came down again and again a figure descended. But this figure moved. The rope swayed and oscillated. The figure came down a good halfway to the ground. It paused, and then descended with much movement to two-thirds of the way from the top.

There something seemed to alarm it. It began to rise with violent writhings of the rope. It climbed.

There was a crackling noise. A stun-pistol. The figure seemed to climb more frantically. More cracklings. They were stun-pistol charges and there were tiny sparks where they hit. The dangling figure seemed convulsed. It went limp, but it did not fall. More charges poured into it. It hung motionless halfway up the wall of the embassy.

Movements began in the darkness. Men appeared, talking in low tones and straining their eyes toward the now motionless figure. They gathered underneath it. One went off at a run, carrying a message. Someone of authority arrived, panting. There was more low-toned argument. More and still more men appeared. There were forty or fifty figures at the base of the wall.

One of those figures began to climb the rope hand over hand. He reached the motionless object. He swore in a shocked voice. He was shushed from below. He let the figure drop. It made no sound when it landed.

Then there was a rushing, as the guards about the embassy went furiously back to their proper posts to keep anybody from slipping out. The two men who remained swore bitterly over a dummy made of' old clothes and pillows.

Hoddan was then some blocks away. He suffered painful doubt about the note ostensibly from Nedda. The guards about the embassy would have tried to catch him in any case, but it did seem very plausible that the note had been sent him to get him to try to climb down the wall. On the other hand, a false descent of a palpably dummy-like dummy had been plausible too. He'd drawn all the guards to one spot by his seeming doubt and by testing out their vigilance with a dummy. The only thing improbable in his behavior had been that after testing their vigilance with a dummy, he'd made use of it.

A fair distance away, he turned sedately into a narrow lane between buildings. This paralleled another lane serving the home of a girl friend of Nedda's. The note had named the garden behind that other girl's home as a rendezvous. But Hoddan was not going to that garden. He wanted to make sure. If the cops had forged the note…

He judged his position carefully. If he climbed this tree… kind of the city-planners of Walden to use trees so lavishly…if he climbed this tree he could look into the garden where Nedda, in theory, waited in tears. He climbed it. He sat astride a thick limb and considered further. Presently he brought out his wave projector. There was deepest darkness hereabouts. Trees and shrubbery were blacker than their surroundings. But there was reason for suspicion. Neither in the house of Nedda's girl friend, nor in the nearer house between, was there a single lighted window.

Hoddan adjusted the wave guide and pressed the stud of his instrument. He pointed it carefully into the nearer garden.

A man grunted in a surprised tone. There was a stirring. A man swore. The words seemed inappropriate to a citizen merely taking a breath of evening air.

Hoddan frowned. The note from Nedda seemed to have been a forgery. To make sure, he readjusted the wave guide to project a thin but fan-shaped beam. He aimed again. Painstakingly, he traversed the area in which men would have been posted to jump him. If Nedda were there, she would feel no effect. If police lay in wait, they would notice at once.

They did. A man howled. Two men yelled together. Somebody bellowed. Somebody squealed. Someone in charge of the flares made ready to give light for the police was so startled by a strange sensation that he jerked the cord. An immense, cold-white brilliance appeared. The garden where Nedda definitely was not present became bathed in incandescence. Light spilled over the wall of one garden into the next and disclosed a squirming mass of police in the nearer garden also. Some of them leaped wildly and ungracefully while clawing behind them. Some stood still and struggled desperately to accomplish something to their rear, while others gazed blankly at them until Hoddan swung his instrument their way, also.

A man tore off his pants and struggled over the wall to get away from something intolerable. Others imitated him. Some removed their trousers before they fled, but others tried to get them off while fleeing! The latter did not fare too well. Mostly they stumbled and other men fell over them.

Hoddan let the confusion mount past any unscrambling, and then slid down the tree and joined in the rush. With the glare in the air behind him, he only feigned to stumble over one figure after another. Once he grunted as he scorched his own fingers. But he came out of the lane with a dozen stun-pistols, mostly uncomfortably warm, as trophies of the ambush.

As they cooled off he stowed them away in his belt and pockets, strolling away down the tree-lined sheet. Behind him, cops realized their trouserless condition and appealed plaintively to householders to notify headquarters of their state.

Hoddan did not feel particularly disillusioned, somehow. It occurred to him, even, that this particular event was likely to help him get off of Walden. If he was to leave against the cops' will, he needed to have them at less than top efficiency. And men who have had their pants scorched off them are not apt to think too clearly. Hoddan felt a certain confidence increase in his mind. He'd worked the thing out very nicely. If ionization made air a high-resistance conductor, then an ionizing beam would make a high-resistance short between the power terminals of a stun-pistol. With the power a stun-pistol carried, that short would get hot. So would the pistol. It would get hot enough, in fact, to scorch cloth in contact with it. Which had happened.

If the effect had been produced in the soles of policemen's feet, Hoddan would have given every cop a hot-foot. But since they carried their sun-pistols in their hip-pockets…

The thought of Nedda diminished his satisfaction. The note could be pure forgery, or the police could have learned about it through the treachery of the servant she sent to the embassy with it. It would be worth while to know. He headed toward the home of her father. If she were loyal to him, it would complicate things considerably. But he felt it necessary to find out.

He neared the spot where Nedda lived. This was an especially desirable residential area. The houses were large and gracefully designed, and the gardens were especially lush. Presently he heard music ahead. He went on. He came to a place where strolling citizens had paused under the trees to listen to the melody and the sound of voices that accompanied it. The music and festivity was in Nedda's name. She was having a party, on the night of the terrible day in which he'd been framed for life imprisonment.

It was a shock. Then there was a rush of vehicles, and police trucks were disgorging cops before the door. They formed a cordon about the house, and some knocked and were admitted in haste. Then Hoddan nodded dourly to himself.

His escape from the embassy was now known. No less certainly, the failure of the trap Nedda's note had baited had been reported. The police were now turning the whole city into a trap for one Bron Hoddan. Soon they'd have cops from other cities pouring in to aid in the search. And certainly and positively they'd take every measure they could to keep him from getting back to the embassy.

It was a situation that would have appalled Hoddan only that morning. Now, though, he only shook his head sadly. He moved on. Somehow he must get back into the embassy.

It was not far from Nedda's house to a public-safety kiosk. He entered it. It was unattended, of course. It was simply an out-of-door installation where cops could be summoned, fires reported, or emergencies described by citizens independently of the regular home communicators. It had occurred to Hoddan that the planetary authorities would be greatly pleased to hear of a situation, in a place, that would seem to hint at his presence. There were all sorts of public services that would be delighted to operate impressively in their own lines. There were bureaus which would rejoice at a chance to show off their efficiency.

He used his micro-wave generator—which at short enough range would short-circuit anything—upon the apparatus in the kiosk. It was perfectly simple, if one knew how. He worked with a sort of tender thoroughness, shorting this item, shorting that, giving this frantic emergency call, stating that baseless lie. When he went out of the kiosk he walked briskly toward an appointment he had made.

And presently the murmur of the city at night had new sounds added to it. They began as a faint, confused clamor at the edges of the city. The uproar moved central-ward and grew louder. There were clanging bells and sirens and beeper-horns warning all non-official vehicles to keep out of the way. On the raised-up express-way snorting metal monsters rushed with squealing excitement. On the fragrant lesser streets, smaller vehicles rushed with pro-portionately louder howlings. Police trucks poured out of their cubbyholes and plunged valiantly through the dark. Broadcast units signaled emergency and cut off the air to make the placid ether waves available to authority.

All these noises and all this tumult moved toward a single point. The outer parts of the city regained their former quiet. But in the mid-city area the noise of racing vehicles clamoring for right-of-way grew louder and louder. The sound was deafening as the vehicles converged on the large open square in front of the Interstellar Embassy. From every street and avenue fire-fighting equipment poured into that square. In between and behind, hoot-ing loudly for precedence, were the police trucks. Emergency ve-hicles of all the civic bureaus appeared, all of them with immense conviction of their importance.

It was a very large, open square, that space before the embas-sy. From its edge, the monument to the first settlers in the center looked small. But even that vast plaza filled up with trucks of ev-ery imaginable variety, from the hose towers which could throw streams of water four hundred feet straight up, to the miniature trouble-wagons of Electricity Supply. Staff cars of fire and police and sanitary services crowded each other and bumped fenders with tree-surgeon trucks prepared to move fallen trees, and with public-address trucks ready to lend stentorian tones to any voice of authority.

But there was no situation except that there was no situation. There was no fire. There was no riot. There were not even stray dogs for the pound-wagons to pursue, nor broken water mains for the water department technicians to shut off and repair. There was nothing for anybody to do but ask everybody else what the hell they were doing there, and presently to swear at each other for cluttering up the way.

The din of arriving horns and sirens had stopped, and a mut-ter of profanity was developing, when a last vehicle arrived. It was an ambulance, an it came purposefully out of a side avenue and swung toward a particular place as if it knew exactly what it was about. When its way was blocked, it hooted impatiently for passage. Its lights blinked violently red, demanding clearance. A giant fire-fighting unit pulled aside. The ambulance ran past and hooted at a cluster of police trucks. They made way for it. It blared at a gathering of dismounted, irritated truck personnel. It made its way through them. It moved in a straight line for the gate of the Interstellar Embassy.

A hundred yards from that gate, its horn blatted irritably at the car of the acting head of municipal police. That car obediently made way for it.

The ambulance rolled briskly up to the very gate of the embassy. There it stopped. A figure got down from the driver's seat and walked purposefully in the gate.

Thereafter nothing happened at all until a second figure rolled and toppled itself out on the ground from the seat beside the ambulance driver's. That figure kicked and writhed on the ground. A policeman went to find out what was the matter.

It was the ambulance driver. Not the one who'd driven the ambulance to the embassy gate, but the one who should have. He was bound hand and foot and not too tightly gagged.

When released he swore vividly while panting that he had been captured and bound by somebody who said he was Bron Hoddan and was in a hurry to get back to the Interstellar Embassy.

There was no uproar. Those to whom Hoddan's name had meaning were struck speechless with rage. The fury of the police was even too deep for tears.

But Bron Hoddan, back in the quarters assigned him in the embassy, unloaded a dozen cooled-off stun-pistols from his pockets and sent word to the Ambassador that he was back, and that the note ostensibly from Nedda had actually been a police trap.

Getting ready to retire, he reviewed his situation. In some respects it was not too bad. All but Nedda's share in trying to trap him, and having a party the same night. He stared morosely at the wall. Then he saw, very simply, that she mightn't have known even of his arrest. She lived a highly sheltered life. Her father could have had her kept in complete ignorance.

He cheered immediately. This would be his last night on Walden, if he were lucky. Already vague plans revolved in his mind. Yes...he'd achieve splendid things; he'd grow rich; he'd come back and marry that delightful girl, Nedda; and then end as a great man. Already, today, he'd done a number of things worth doing, and on the whole he'd done them well.

# CHAPTER III

When dawn broke over the capital city of Walden, the sight was appropriately glamorous. There were shining towers and the curving tree-bordered ways, above which innumerable small birds flew. The dawn, in fact, was heralded by chirpings everywhere. During the darkness there had been a deep-toned humming sound, audible all over the city. That was the landing-grid in operation out at the spaceport, letting clown a huge liner from Rigel, Cetis, and the Nearer Rim. Presently it would take off for Krim, Darth, and the Coal-sack Stars, and if Hoddan were lucky he would be on it. At the earliest part of the day there was only tranquility over the city and the square and the Interstellar Embassy.

At the gate of the embassy enclosure, staff members piled up boxes and bales and parcels for transport to the spaceport and thence to destinations whose names were practically songs. There were dispatches to Delil, where the Interstellar Diplomatic Service had a sector headquarters, and there were packets of embassy-stamped invoices for Lohala and Tralee and Famagusta. There were boxes for Sind and Maja, and metal-bound cases for Kent. The early explorers of this part of the galaxy had christened the huge suns with the names of little villages and territories back on Earth.

The sound of the stacking of freight parcels was crisp and distinct in the morning hush. The dew deposited during the night had not yet dried from the pavement of the square. Damp, unhappy figures loafed nearby. They were the secret police, as yet unrelieved after a night's vigil about the embassy's rugged wall. They were sleepy, and their clothing stuck soggily to them, and none of them had anything warm to eat for many hours. They had not, either, anything to look forward to from their superiors. Hoddan was again in sanctuary inside the embassy they'd guarded so ineptly through the dark. He'd gotten out without their leave, and had made a number of their fellows quite uncomfortable. Then he had made all the police and municipal authorities ridiculous by the manner of his return. The police guards about the embassy were positively not in a cheery mood. But one of them saw an embassy servant he knew. He'd stood the man drinks, in times past, to establish a contact that might be useful. He smiled and beckoned to the man.

The embassy servant came briskly to him, rubbing his hands after having put a moderately heavy case of documents on top of the waiting pile.

"That Hoddan," said the plainclothesman, attempting hearty ruefulness, "he certainly put it over on us last night!"

The servant nodded.

"Look," said the plainclothesman," there could be something in it for you if you—hm—wanted to make a little extra money."

The servant looked regretful.

"No chance," he said. "He's leaving today."

The plainclothesman jumped.

"Today?"

"For Darth," said the embassy servant. "The ambassador's shipping him off on the spaceliner that came in last night."

The plainclothesman dithered.

"How's he going to get to the spaceport?"

"I wouldn't know," said the servant. "They've figured out some way. I could use a little extra money, too."

He lingered, but the plainclothesman was staring at the innocent, inviolable parcels about to leave the embassy for distant parts. He took note of sizes and descriptions. No. Not yet. But if Hoddan was leaving, he had to leave the embassy. If he left the embassy...

The plainclothesman bolted. He made a breathless report by the portable communicator. He told what the embassy servant had said. Orders came back to him. Orders were given in all directions. Somebody was going to distinguish himself by catching Hoddan, and undercover politics worked to decide who it should be. Even the job of guarding the embassy became desirable. So fresh, alert plainclothesmen arrived. They were bright eyed and bushy tailed, and they took over. Weary, hungry men yielded up their posts. They went home. The man who'd gotten the clue went home too, disgruntled because he wouldn't be allowed a share in the credit for Hoddan's actual capture. But he was glad of it later.

Inside the embassy, Hoddan finished his breakfast with the ambassador.

"I'm giving you," said the ambassador, "a letter to that character on Darth. I told you about him. He's some sort of nobleman and has need of an electronic engineer. On Darth they're rare to nonexistent. But his letter wasn't too specific."

"I remember," agreed Hoddan. "I'll look him up. Thanks."

"Somehow," said the ambassador, "I cherish unreasonable hopes for you, Hoddan. A psychologist would say that your group identification is low and your cyclothymia practically a minus quantity, while your ergic tension is pleasingly high. He'd mean that with reasonable good fortune you will raise more hell than most. I wish you that good fortune. And Hoddan—"

"Yes?"

"I urge you not to be vengeful," explained the ambassador, "but I do hope you won't be too forgiving of these characters who'd have jailed you for life. You've scared them badly. It's very good for them. Anything more you can do along that line will be really a kindness, even though it will positively not be appreciated. But it'll be well worth doing. I say this because I like the way you plan things. And any time I can be of service…"

"Thanks," said Hoddan. "Now I'd better get going for the spaceport." He'd write Nedda from Darth. "I'll get set for it."

He rose. The ambassador stood up, too.

"I like the way you plan things," he repeated appreciatively. "We'll check over that box."

They left the embassy dining room together.

It was well after sunrise when Hoddan finished his breakfast, and the bright and watchful new plainclothesmen were very much on the alert outside. By this time the sunshine had lost its early ruddy tint, and the trees about the city were vividly green, and the sky had become appropriately blue—as the skies on all human-occupied planets are. There was the beginning of traffic.

Some was routine movement of goods and vehicles. But some was special.

For example, the trucks which came to carry the embassy shipment to the spaceport. They were perfectly ordinary trucks, hired in a perfectly ordinary way by the ambassador's secretary. They came trundling across the square and into the embassy gate. The ostentatiously loafing plainclothesmen could look in and see the waiting parcels loaded on them. The first truck load was quite unsuspicious. There was no package in the lot which could have held a man even the most impossibly cramped of positions.

But the police took no chances. Ten blocks from the embassy the cops stopped it and verified the licenses and identities of the driver and his helper. This was a moderately lengthy business. While it went on, plainclothesmen walked over the packages in the truck's body and put stethoscopes to any of more than one cubic foot capacity.

They waved the truck on. Meanwhile the second truck was loading up. And those watching, saw that the last item to be loaded was a large box which hadn't been seen before. It was carried with some care, and it was marked fragile, put into place and wedged fast with other parcels.

The plainclothesmen looked at each other with anticipatory glee. One of them reported the last large box with almost lyric enthusiasm. When the second truck left the embassy with the large box, a police truck came innocently out of nowhere and just happened to be going the same way. Ten blocks away, again the truckload of embassy parcels was flagged down and its driver's license and identity was verified. A plainclothesman put a stethoscope on the questionable case. He beamed, and made a suitable signal.

The truck went on, while zestful, Machiavellian plans took effect.

Five blocks farther, an unmarked empty truck came hurtling out of a side street, sideswiped the truck from the embassy, and went careening away down the street without stopping. The trailing police truck made no attempt at pursuit. Instead, it stopped helpfully by the truck which had been hit. A wheel was hopelessly gone. So uniformed police, with conspicuously happy expressions, cleared a space around the stalled truck and stood guard over the parcels under diplomatic seal. With eager helpfulness, they sent for other transportation for the embassy's shipment.

A sneeze was heard from within the mass of guarded freight, and the policemen shook hands with each other. When substitute trucks came—there were two of them—they loaded one high with embassy parcels and sent it off to the spaceport with their blessings. There remained just one, single, large box to be put on the second vehicle. They bumped it on the ground, and a startled grunt came from within.

There was an atmosphere of innocent enjoyment all about as the police tenderly loaded this large box on a second truck. Strangely, they did not head directly for the spaceport. The police carefully explained this to each other in loud voices. Then some of them were afraid the box hadn't heard, so they knocked on it. The box coughed, and it seemed hilariously amusing to the policemen that the contents of a freight parcel should cough. They expressed deep concern and—addressing the box—explained that they were taking it to the Detention Building, where they would give it some cough medicine.

The box swore at them, despairingly. They howled with childish laughter, and assured the box that after they had opened it and given it cough medicine they would close it again very carefully—leaving the diplomatic seal unbroken—and deliver it to the spaceport so it could go on its way.

The box swore again, luridly. The truck which carried it hastened. The box teetered and bumped and jounced with the swift motion of the vehicle that carried it and all the police around it. Bitter, enraged, and highly unprintable language came from within.

The police were charmed. When the Detention Building gate opened for it, and closed again behind it, there was a welcoming committee in the courtyard. It included a jailer with a bandaged head and a look of vengeful satisfaction on his face, and no less than the three guards who had been given baths by a high-pressure hose. They wore unamiable expressions.

And then, while the box swore very bitterly, somebody tenderly loosened a plank—being careful not to disturb the diplomatic seal—and pulled it away with a triumphant gesture. Then all the police could look into the box. And they did.

Then there was a dead silence, except for the voice that came from a two-way communicator set inside.

"And now," said the voice from the box, "and now we take our leave of the planet Walden and its happy police force, who wave to us as our spaceliner lifts toward the skies. The next sound you hear will be that of their lamentations at our departure."

But the next sound was a howl of fury. The police were very much disappointed to find that it hadn't been Hoddan in the box, but only one-half of a two-way communication pair. Hoddan *had* coughed, sneezed and sworn at them, but from the other instrument somewhere else. Now he signed off.

The spaceliner was not lifting off just yet. It was still solidly aground in the center of the landing-grid. Hoddan had bade farewell to his audience from the floor of the ambassador's car, which at that moment was safely within the extra-territorial circle about the spaceship. He turned off the set and got up and brushed himself off. He got out of the car. The ambassador followed him and shook his hand.

"You have a touch," said the ambassador sedately. "You seem inspired at times, Hoddan! You have a gift for infuriating constituted authority. You may go far!"

He shook hands again and watched Hoddan walk into the lift which raised him to the entrance port of the spaceliner.

Twenty minutes later the force-fields of the giant landing-grid lifted the liner smoothly out to space. The vessel went out to five planetary diameters, where its Lawlor drive could take hold of relatively unstressed space. There the ship jockeyed for line, and then there was that curious, momentary disturbance of all one's sensations which was the effect of the over-drive field going on. Then everything was normal again, except that the liner was speeding for the planet Krim at something more than thirty times the speed of light.

Normalcy extended through all the galaxy so far inhabited by men. There were worlds on which there was peace, and worlds on which there was tumult. There were busy, restful young worlds, and languid, weary old ones. From the Near Rim to the farthest of occupied systems, planets circled their suns, and men lived on them, and every man took himself seriously and did not quite believe that the universe had existed before he was born or would long survive his loss.

Time passed. Comets let out vast streamers like bridal veils and swept toward and around their suns. The liner bearing Hoddan sped through the void.

In time it made a landfall on the Planet Krim. He went aground and observed the spaceport city. It was new and bustling with tall buildings and traffic jams and a feverish conviction that the purpose of living was to earn more money this year than last. Its spaceport was chaotically busy. Hoddan had time for swift sight-seeing in one city only. He saw slums and gracious public buildings, and went back to the spaceport and the liner which then rose upon the landing-grid's forcefields until Krim was a great round ball below it. Then there was again a jockeying for line, and the liner winked out of sight and was again journeying at thirty times the speed of light.

Again time passed. In one of the most remote galaxies a super-nova flamed, and on a rocky, barren world a small living thing squirmed experimentally—to mankind the one event was just as important as the other.

But presently the liner from Walden via Krim appeared on Darth as the tiniest of shimmering pearly specks against the blue. To the north and east and west of the spaceport, rugged mountains rose steeply. Patches of snow showed here and there, and naked rock reared boldly in spurs and precipices. But there were trees on all the lower slopes, and there was not really a timber line.

The spaceliner increased in size, descending toward the landing-grid. The grid itself was a monstrous lattice of steel, a half-mile high and enclosing a circle not less in diameter. It filled the larger part of the level valley floor, and horned *duryas* and what Hoddan later learned were horses grazed in it. The animals paid no attention to the deep humming noise the grid made in its operation.

The ship seemed the size of a pea. Presently it was the size of an apple. Then it was the size of a basketball, and then it swelled enormously and put out spidery metal legs with large splay metal feet on which it alighted and settled gently to the ground. The humming stopped.

There were shoutings. Whips cracked. Straining, horn-tossing *duryas* heaved and dragged something, very deliberately, out from between warehouses and under the arches of the grid. There were two dozen of the *duryas,* and despite the shouts and whip cracking they moved with a stubborn slowness. It took a long time for the object with the big clumsy wheels to reach a spot below the spacecraft. Then it took longer, seemingly, for brakes to be set on each wheel, and then for the draft animals to be arranged to pull as two teams against each other.

More shoutings and whip-crackings. A long, slanting, ladderlike arm rose. It teetered, and a man with a vivid purple cloak rose with it at its very end. The ship's airlock opened and a crewman threw a rope. The purple-cloaked man caught it and made it fast. From somewhere inside the ship, the line was hauled in. The end of the landing ramp touched the sill of the airlock. Somebody made these fast and the purple-cloaked man triumphantly entered the ship.

There was a pause. Men loaded carts with cargo to be sent to other remote planets. In the airlock, Bron Hoddan stepped to the unloading-ramp and descended to the ground. He was the only passenger. He had barely reached a firm footing when objects followed him. His own ship bag and then parcels, bales, boxes, and other such nondescript items of freight. For a mere five minutes the flow of freight continued. Darth was not an important center of trade.

Hoddan stared incredulously at the town outside one side of the grid. It was only a town, and was almost a village. Its houses had steep, gabled roofs, of which some seemed to be tile and others thatch. Its buildings leaned over the narrow streets, which were unpaved. They looked like mud. And there was not a power-driven ground-vehicle anywhere in sight, nor anything man-made in the air.

Great carts trailed out to the unloading-belt. They dumped bales of skins and ingots of metal, and more bales and more ingots. Those objects rode up to the airlock and vanished. Hoddan was ignored. He felt that without great care he might be crowded back into the reversed loading-belt and be carried back into the ship.

The loading process ended. The man with the purple cloak, who'd ridden the teetering ladder up, reappeared and came striding grandly down to ground. Somebody cast off, above. Ropes writhed, fell and dangled. The ship's airlock door closed.

There was a vast humming sound. The ship lifted sedately. It seemed to hover momentarily over the group of *duryas* and humans in the center of the grid's enclosure. But it was hovering. It shrank. It was rising in an absolutely vertical line. It dwindled to the size of a basketball and then an apple. Then to the size of a pea. And then that pea diminished until the spaceship from Krim, Walden, Cetis, Rigel and the Nearer Rim had become the size of a dust mote and then could not be seen at all. But one knew that it was going on to Lohala and Tralee and Famagusta and the Coalsack Stars.

Hoddan shrugged and began to trudge toward the warehouses. The *durya-drawn* landing-ramp began to roll slowly in the same direction. Carts and wagons loaded the stuff discharged from the ship. Creaking, plodding, with the curved horns of the *duryas* rising and falling, the wagons overtook Hoddan and passed him. He saw his ship bag on one of the carts. It was a gift from the Interstellar Ambassador on Walden. He'd assured Hoddan that there was a fund for the assistance of political refugees, and that the bag and its contents was normal. But in addition to this, Hoddan had a number of stun-pistols, formerly equipment of the police department of Walden's capital city.

He followed his bag to a warehouse. Arrived there, he found the bag surrounded by a group of whiskered Darthian characters wearing felt pants and large sheath knives. They had opened the bag and were in the act of ferocious dispute about who should get what of its contents. Incidentally they argued over the stun-pistols, which looked like weapons but weren't because nothing happened when one pulled the trigger. Hoddan grimaced. They'd been in store on the liner during the voyage. Normally they picked up a trickle charge from broadcast power, on Walden, but there was no broadcast power on the liner, nor on Darth. They'd leaked their charges and were quite useless. The one in his pocket would be useless, too.

He grimaced again and swerved to the building where the landing-grid controls must be. He opened the door and went in. The interior was smoky and vile-smelling, but the equipment was wholly familiar. Two unshaven men in violently colored shirts, languidly played cards. Only one, a redhead, paid attention to the controls of the landing-grid. He watched dials. As Hoddan pushed his way in, he threw a switch and yawned. The ship was five diameters out from Darth, and he'd released it from the landing-grid fields. He turned and saw Hoddan.

"What the hell do you want?" he demanded sharply.

"A few kilowatts," said Hoddan. The redhead's manner was not amiable.

"Get outta here!" he barked.

The transformers and snaky cables leading to relays outside—all were clear as print to Hoddan. He moved confidently toward an especially understandable panel, pulling out his stun-pistol and briskly breaking back the butt for charging. He shoved the pistol butt to contact with two terminals devised for another purpose, and the pistol slipped for an instant and a blue spark flared.

"Quit that!" roared the man. The unshaven men pushed back from their game of cards. One of them stood up, smiling unpleasantly.

The stun-pistol clicked. Hoddan withdrew it from charging-contact, flipped the butt shut, and turned toward the three men. Two of them charged him suddenly—the redhead and the unpleasant smiler.

The stun-pistol hummed. The redhead howled. He'd been hit in the hand. His unshaven companion buckled in the middle and fell to the floor. The third man backed away in panic, automatically raising his arms in surrender.

Hoddan saw no need for further action. He nodded graciously and went out of the control building, swinging the recharged pistol in his hand. In the warehouse, argument still raged over his

possessions. He went in. Nobody looked at him. The casual ap-
propriation of unguarded property was apparently a social norm,
here. The man in the purple cloak was insisting furiously that he
was a Darthian gentleman and he'd have his share—or else!

"Those things," said Hoddan, "are mine. Put them back."

Faces turned to him, expressing shocked surprise. A man in
dirty yellow pants stood up with a suit of Hoddan's underwear
and a pair of shoes. He moved to depart with great dignity.

The stun-pistol buzzed. He leaped and howled and fled.

There was a concerted gasp of outrage. Men leaped to their
feet. Large knives came out of elaborate holsters. Figures in all
the colors of the rainbow—all badly soiled—roared their indignation and charged at Hoddan. They waved knives as they came.

He held down the stun-pistol trigger and traversed the rushing
men. The whining buzz of the weapon was inaudible, at first, but
before he released the trigger it was plainly to be heard. Then
there was silence. His attackers formed a very untidy heap on the
floor. They breathed stertorously. Hoddan began to retrieve his
possessions. He rolled a man over, for this purpose; a pair of very
blue, apprehensive eyes stared at him. Their owner had stumbled
over one man and been stumbled over by others. He gazed up at
Hoddan, speechless.

"Hand me that, please," said Hoddan. He pointed.

The man in the purple cloak obeyed, shaking. Hoddan completed the recovery of all his belongings. He turned. The man in
the purple cloak winced and closed his eyes.

"Hm," said Hoddan. He needed information. He spoke to the
man: "I have a letter of introduction to one Don Loris. Would you
have any idea how I could reach him?"

The man in the purple cloak gaped at Hoddan.

"He is…is my chieftain," he said, aghast. "I—am Thal, his
most trusted retainer." Then he practically wailed. "You must be
the man I was sent to meet! He sent me to learn if you came on
the ship! I should have fought by your side! This is disgrace!"

"It's disgraceful," agreed Hoddan grimly. But he, who had
been born and raised in a space-pirate community, was not too
critical of others. "Let it go. How do I find him?"

"I should take you!" complained Thal bitterly. "But you have killed all these men. Their friends and chieftains are honor bound to cut your throat! And you shot Merk, but he ran away, and he will be summoning his friends to come and kill you now! This is shame!" Then he said hopefully, "Your strange weapon…how many men can you fight? If fifty, we may live to ride away. If more, we may even reach Don Loris' castle. How many?"

"We'll see what we see," said Hoddan dourly. "But I'd better charge these other pistols. You can come with me, or wait. I haven't killed these men. They're only stunned. They'll come around presently."

He went out of the warehouse, carrying the bag which was again loaded with uncharged stun-pistols. He went back to the grid's control-room. He pushed it open and entered for the second time. The redhead swore and grabbed at his hand. The man who'd smiled unpleasantly lay in a heap on the floor. The second unshaven man jittered visibly at sight of Hoddan.

"I'm back," said Hoddan politely, "for more kilowatts." He put his bag conveniently close to the terminals at which his pistols could be recharged. He snapped open a pistol butt and presented it to the electric contacts.

"Quaint customs you have here," he said conversationally. "Robbing a newcomer. Resenting his need for a few watts of power that comes free from the sky." The stun-pistol clicked. He snapped the butt shut and opened another, which he placed in contact for charging. "Making him act," he added acidly, "with manners as bad as the local ones. Going at him with knives so he has to be resentful in his turn." The second stun-pistol clicked. He closed it and began to charge a third. He said severely, "Innocent tourists—relatively innocent ones, anyhow—are not likely to be favorably impressed with Darth!" He had the charging process going swiftly now. He began to charge a fourth weapon. "It's particularly bad manners," he added sternly, "to stand there grinding your teeth at me while your friend behind the desk crawls after an old-fashioned chemical gun to shoot me with."

He snapped the fourth pistol shut and went after the man who'd dropped down behind a desk. He came upon that man, hopelessly panicked, just as his hands closed on a clumsy gun that was supposed to set off a chemical explosive to propel a metal bullet.

"Don't!" said Hoddan severely. "If I have to shoot you at this range, you'll have blisters!"

He took the weapon out of the other man's hands. He went back and finished charging the rest of the pistols.

He returned most of them to his bag, though he stuck others in his belt and pockets to the point where he looked like the fiction-tape version of a space-pirate. He moved to the door. As a last thought, he picked up the bullet-firing weapon.

"There's only one spaceship here a month," he observed politely, "so I'll be around. If you want to get in touch with me, ask Don Loris. I'm going to visit him while I look over the professional opportunities on Darth."

He went out once more. Somehow he felt more cheerful than a half-hour since, when he'd landed as the only passenger from the spaceliner. Then he'd felt ignored and lonely and friendless on a strange and primitive world. He still had no friends, but he had already acquired some enemies and therefore material for more or less worthwhile achievement. He surveyed the sunlit scene about him from the control-room door.

Thal, the purple-cloaked man, had brought two shaggy-haired animals around to the door of the warehouse. Hoddan later learned that they were horses. He was in furious haste to mount one of them. As he climbed up, small bright metal disks cascaded from a pocket. He tried to stop the flow of money as he got feverishly into the saddle.

From the small town a mob of some fifty mounted men plunged toward the landing-grid. They wore garments of yellow and blue and magenta. They waved huge knives and made bloodthirsty noises. Thal saw them and bolted, riding one horse and towing the other by a lead rope. It happened that his line of retreat passed by where Hoddan stood. Hoddan held up his hand. Thal reined in.

"Mount!" Thal cried hoarsely. "Mount and ride!"

Hoddan passed him the chemical gun. Thal seized it frantically.

"Hurry!" he panted. "Don Loris would have my throat cut if I deserted you! Mount and ride!"

Hoddan painstakingly fastened his bag to the saddle of his horse. He unfastened the lead rope. He'd noticed that Thal pulled in the leather reins to stop the horse. He'd seen that he kicked it furiously to urge it on. He deduced that one steered the animal by pulling on one strap or the other. He climbed clumsily to a seat.

There was a howl from the racing, mounted men. They waved their knives and yelled in zestful anticipation of murder.

Hoddan pulled on a rein. His horse turned obediently. He kicked it. The animal broke into a run toward the rushing mob. The jolting motion amazed Hoddan. One could not shoot straight while being shaken up like this! He dragged back on the reins. The horse stopped.

"Come!" yelled Thal despairingly. "This way! Quick!"

Hoddan got out a stun-pistol. Sitting erect, frowning a little in his concentration, he began to take pot shots at the advancing men.

Three of them got close enough to be blistered when stun-pistol bolts hit them. Others toppled from their saddles at distances ranging from one hundred yards to twenty. A good dozen, however, saw what was happening in time to swerve their mounts and hightail it away. But there were eighteen luridly-tinted heaps of garments on the ground inside the landing-grid. Two or three of them squirmed and swore. Hoddan had partly missed, on them. He heard the chemical weapon booming thunderously. Now that victory was won, Thal was shooting. Hoddan held up his hand for cease-fire. Thal rode up beside him, not quite believing what he'd seen.

"Wonderful," he said shakily. "Wonderful! Don Loris will be pleased! He will give me gifts for my help to you. This is a great fight! We will be great men, after this!"

"Then let's go and brag," said Hoddan.

Thal was shocked.

"You need me," he said. "It is fortunate that Don Loris chose me to fight beside you!"

He sent his horse trotting toward the unconscious men on the ground. He alighted. Hoddan saw him happily and publicly pick the pockets of the stun-gun's victims. He came back beaming.

"We will be famous!" he said zestfully. "Two against thirty, and some ran away!" he gloated. "And it was a good haul! We share, of course, because we are companions."

"Is it the custom," asked Hoddan mildly, "to loot defenseless men?"

"But of course!" said Thal. "How else can a gentleman live, if he has no chieftain to give him presents? You defeated them, so of course you take their possessions!"

"Ah, yes," said Hoddan. "To be sure!"

He rode on. The road was a mere horse track. Presently it was less than that. He saw a frowning, battlemented stronghold away off to the left. Thal openly hoped that somebody would come from that castle and try to charge them toll for riding over their lords land. After Hoddan had knocked them over with the stun-pistols, Thal would add to the heavy weight of coins already in his possession.

It did not look promising, in a way. But just before sunset, Hoddan saw three tiny bright lights flash across the sky from west to east. They moved in formation and at identical speeds. Hoddan knew a spaceship in orbit when he saw one. He bristled, and muttered under his breath.

"What's that?" asked Thal. "What did you say?"

"I said," said Hoddan dourly, "that I've got to do something about Walden. When they get an idea in their heads..."

# CHAPTER IV

According to the fiction-tapes, the colonized worlds of the galaxy vary wildly from each other. In cold and unromantic fact, it isn't so. Space travel is too cheap and sol-type solar systems too numerous to justify the settlement of hostile worlds. Therefore Bron Hoddan encountered no remarkable features in the landscape of Darth as he rode through the deepening night. There was grass, bushes, trees, birds, and various other commonplace living things whose ancestors had been dumped on Darth some centuries before. The ecological system had worked itself out strictly by hit-or-miss, but the result was not unusual. There was, though, the unfamiliar star-pattern. Hoddan tried to organize it in his mind. He knew where the sun had set, which would be west. He asked the latitude of the Darthian spaceport. Thal did not know it. He asked about major geographical features—seas, continents, and so on. Thal had no ideas on the subject.

Hoddan fumed. He hadn't worried about such things on Walden. Of course, on Walden he'd had one friend, Derec, and believed he had a sweetheart, Nedda. There he was lonely and schemed to acquire the admiration of others. He ignored the sky. Here on Darth he had no friends, but there were a number of local citizens now recovering from stun-pistol bolts and yearning to carve him up with large knives. He did not feel lonely, but the instinct to know where he was, was again in operation.

The ground was rocky and far from level. After two hours of riding on a small and wiry horse with no built-in springs, Hoddan hurt in a great many places. He and Thal rode in an indeterminate direction with an irregular scarp of low mountains silhouetted against the unfamiliar stars. A vagrant night wind blew. Thal had said it was a three-hour ride to Don Loris' castle. After something over two of them, he said meditatively:

"I think that if you wish to give me a present I will take it and not make a gift in return. You could give me," he added helpfully, "your share of the plunder from our victims."

"Why?" demanded Hoddan. "Why should I give you a present?"

"If I accepted it," explained Thal, "and make no gift in return, I will become your retainer. Then it will be my obligation as a Darthian gentleman to ride beside you, advise, counsel, and fight in your defense, and generally to uphold your dignity."

"How about Don Loris? Aren't you his retainer?" he asked suspiciously.

"Between the two of us," said Thal, "he's stingy. His presents are not as lavish as they could be. I can make him a return-present of part of the money we won in combat. That frees me of duty to him. Then I could accept the balance of the money from you, and become a retainer of yours."

"Oh," said Hoddan.

"You need a retainer badly," said Thal. "You do not know the customs here. For example, there is enmity between Don Loris and the young Lord Ghek. If the young Lord Ghek is as enterprising as he should be, some of his retainers should be King in wait to cut our throats as we approach Don Loris' stronghold."

"Hm," said Hoddan grimly. But Thal seemed undisturbed. "This system of gifts and presents sounds complicated. Why doesn't Don Loris simply give you so much a year, or week, or whatnot?"

Thal made a shocked sound.

"That would be pay! A Darthian gentleman does not serve for pay! To offer it would be insult!" Then he said, "Listen!"

He reined in. Hoddan clumsily followed his example. After a moment or two Thal clucked to his horse and started off again.

"It was nothing," he said regretfully. "I hoped we were riding into an ambush."

Hoddan grunted. It could be that he was being told a tall tale. But back at the spaceport, the men who came after him waving large knives had seemed sincere enough.

"Why should we be ambushed?" he asked. "And why do you hope for it?"

"Your weapons would destroy our enemies," said Thal placidly, "and the pickings would be good." He added, "We should be ambushed because the Lady Fani refused to marry the Lord Ghek. She is Don Loris' daughter, and to refuse to marry a man is naturally a deadly insult. So he should ravage Don Loris' lands at every opportunity until he gets a chance to carry off the Lady Fani and marry her by force. That is the only way the insult can be wiped out."

"I see," said Hoddan ironically.

He didn't. The two horses topped a rise, and far in the distance there was a yellow light, with a mist above it as of illuminated smoke.

"That is Don Loris' stronghold," said Thal. He sighed. "It looks like we may not be ambushed."

They weren't. It was very dark where the horses forged ahead through brushwood. As they moved onward, the single light became two. They were great bonfires burning in iron cages some forty feet up in the air. Those cages projected from the battlements of a massive, cut-stone wall. There was no light anywhere else.

Thal rode almost under the cressets and shouted upward. A voice answered. Presently a gate clanked open and a black, cave-like opening appeared behind it. Thal rode grandly in, and Hoddan followed.

The gate clanked shut. Torches waved overhead. Hoddan found that he and Thal had ridden into a very tiny courtyard. Twenty feet above them, an inner battlemented wall offered excellent opportunities for the inhabitants of the castle to throw things down at visitors who, after admission, turned out to be undesired.

Thal shouted further identifications, including a boastful and entirely untruthful declaration that he and Hoddan, together, had slaughtered twenty men in one place and thirty in another, and left them lying in their gore.

The voices that replied sounded derisive. Somebody came down a rope and fastened the gate from the inside. With an extreme amount of creaking, an inner gate swung wide. Men came out of it and took the horses. Hoddan dismounted, and it seemed to him that he creaked as loudly as the gate. Thal swaggered, displaying coins he had picked from the pockets of the men the stun-pistols had disabled. He said splendidly to Hoddan:

"I go to announce your coming to Don Loris. These are his retainers. They will give you to drink." He added amiably, "If you were given food, it would be disgraceful to cut your throat."

He disappeared. Hoddan carried his ship bag and followed a man in a dirty pink shirt to a stone-walled room containing a table and a chair. He sat down, relieved. The man in the pink shirt brought him a flagon of wine. He disappeared again.

Hoddan drank the sour wine and brooded. He was very hungry and very tired, and it seemed to him that he had been disillusioned in a new dimension. Morbidly, he remembered a frequently given lecture from his grandfather on Zan.

"It's no use!" his grandfather used to say. "There's not a bit o' use in having brains! All they do is get you into trouble! A lucky idiot's ten times better off than a brainy man with a jinx on him! A smart man starts thinkin', and he thinks himself into a jail cell if his luck is bad, and good luck's wasted on him because it ain't reasonable and he don't believe in it when it happens! It's taken me a lifetime to keep my brains from ruinin' me! No, sir! I hope none o' my descendants inherit my brains I pity 'em if they do!"

Hoddan had been on Darth not more than four hours. In that time he'd found himself robbed, had been the object of two spirited attempts at assassination, had ridden an excruciating number of miles on an unfamiliar animal, and now found himself in a stone dungeon and deprived of food lest feeding him obligate his host not to cut his throat. And he'd gotten into this by himself! He'd chosen it! He'd practically asked for it!

He began strongly to share his grandfather's disillusioned view of brains.

After a long time the door of the cell opened. Thal was back, chastened.

"Don Loris wants to talk to you," he said in a subdued voice. "He's not pleased."

Hoddan took another gulp of the wine. He picked up his ship bag and limped to the door. He decided painfully that he was limping on the wrong leg. He tried the other. No improvement. He really needed to limp on both.

He followed a singularly silent Thal through a long stone corridor and up stone steps until they came to a monstrous hall lit with torches. It was barbarically hung with banners, but it was not exactly a cheery place. At the far end logs burned in a great fireplace.

Don Loris sat in a carved chair beside it; wizened and white-bearded, in a fur-trimmed velvet robe, with a peevish expression on his face.

"My chieftain," said Thal submissively, "here is the engineer from Walden."

Hoddan scowled at Don Loris, whose expression of peevishness did not lighten. He did regard Hoddan with a flicker of interest, however. A stranger who unfeignedly scowls at a feudal lord with no superior and many inferiors, is anyhow a novelty.

"Thal tells me," said Don Loris fretfully, "that you and he, together, slaughtered some dozens of the retainers of my neighbors today. I consider it unfortunate. They may ask me to have the two of you hanged, and it would be impolite to refuse."

Hoddan said truculently:

"I considered it impolite for your neighbors' retainers to march toward me waving large knives."

"Yes," agreed Don Loris impatiently. "I concede that point. It is natural enough to act hastily at such times. But still… How many did you kill?"

"None," said Hoddan curtly. "I shot them with stun-pistols I'd just charged in the control-room of the landing-grid." Don Loris sat up straight.

"Stun-pistols?" he demanded sharply. "You used stun-pistols on Darth?"

"Naturally on Darth," said Hoddan with some tartness. "I was here! But nobody was killed. One or two may be slightly blistered. All of them had their pockets picked by Thal. I understand that is a local custom. There's nothing to worry about."

But Don Loris stared at him, aghast.

"But this is deplorable!" he protested. "Stun-pistols used here? It is the one thing I would have given strict orders to avoid!

My neighbors will talk about it. Some of them may even think about it! You could have used any other weapon, but of all things why did you have to use a stun-pistol?"

"I had one," said Hoddan briefly.

"Horrible!" said Don Loris peevishly. "The worst thing you could possibly have done! I have to disown you. Unmistakably! You'll have to disappear at once. We'll blame it on Ghek's retainers."

"Disappear? Me?" Hoddan exclaimed.

"Vanish," said Don Loris. "I suppose there's no real necessity to cut your throat, but you plainly have to disappear, though it would have been much more discreet if you'd simply gotten killed."

"I was indiscreet to survive?" demanded Hoddan bristling.

"Extremely so!" snapped Don Loris. "Here I had you come all the way from Walden to help arrange a delicate matter, and before you'd traveled even the few miles to my castle—within minutes of landing on Darth—you spoiled everything! I am a reasonable man, but there are the facts! You used stun-pistols, so you have to disappear. I think it generous of me to say only until people on Darth forget that such things exist. But the two of you—oh, for a year or so—there are some fairly cozy dungeons."

Hoddan seethed suddenly. He'd tried to do something brilliant on Walden, and had been framed into jail for life. He'd defended his life and property on Darth, and nearly the same thing popped up as a prospect. Hoddan angrily suspected fate and chance of plain conspiracy against him.

But there was an interruption. A clanking of arms sounded somewhere nearby. Men with long, gruesome, glittering spears came through a doorway. They stood aside. A girl entered the great hall. More spearmen followed her. They stopped by the door. The girl came across the hall.

She was a pretty girl, but Hoddan hardly noticed the fact with so many other things on his mind.

Thal, behind him, said in a quivering voice:

"My Lady Fani, I beg you to plead with your father for his most faithful retainer!"

The girl looked in surprise at him. Her eyes fell on Hoddan. She looked interested. Hoddan, at that moment, was very nearly as disgusted and as indignant as a man could be. He did not look romantically at her—which to the Lady Fani, daughter of that powerful lord, Don Loris, was a novelty. He did not look at her at all. He ground his teeth.

"Don't try to wheedle me, Fani!" snapped Don Loris. "I am a reasonable man, but I indulge you too much—even to allowing you to refuse that young imbecile Ghek, with no end of inconvenience as a result. But I will not have you question my decision about Thal and this Hoddan person!" The girl said pleasantly:

"Of course not, father. But what have they done?"

"The two of them," snapped Don Loris again, "fought twenty men today and defeated all of them! Thal plundered them. Then thirty other men, mounted, tried to avenge the first and they defeated them also! Thal plundered eighteen. And all this was permissible, if unlikely. But they did it with stun-pistols! Everybody will soon be talking of it! They'll know that this Hoddan came to Darth to see me! They'll suspect that I imported new weapons for political purposes! They'll guess at the prettiest scheme I've had these twenty years!"

"But did they really defeat so many?" she asked, marveling. "That's wonderful! And Thal was undoubtedly fighting in defense of someone you'd told him to protect, as a loyal retainer should do. Wasn't he?"

"I wish," fumed her father, "that you would not throw in irrelevancies! I sent him to get Hoddan this afternoon, not to massacre my neighbors' retainers—or rather, not to not massacre them. A little bloodletting would have done no harm, but stun-pistols—"

"He was protecting somebody he was told to protect," said Fani. "And this other man, this—"

"Hoddan, Bron Hoddan," said her father irritably. "Yes. He was protecting himself! Doubtless he thought he did me a service in doing that! But if he'd only let himself get killed quietly, the whole affair would be simplified!"

The Lady Fani said with quiet dignity:

"By the same reasoning, father, it would simplify things greatly if I let the Lord Ghek kidnap me."

"It's not the same thing at all."

"At least," said Fani," I wouldn't have a pack of spearmen following me about like foul-breathed puppies everywhere I go!"

"It's not the same."

"And it's especially unreasonable," continued the Lady Fani with even greater dignity, "when you could put Thal and this Hoddan person on duty to guard me instead. If they can fight twenty and thirty men at once, all by themselves, it doesn't seem to me that you think much of my safety when you want to lock them up somewhere instead of using them to keep your daughter safe from that particularly horrible Ghek!"

Don Loris swore in a cracked voice. Then he said.

"To end the argument I'll think it over. Until tomorrow. Now go away!"

Fani, beaming, rose and kissed him on the forehead. He squirmed. She turned to leave, and beckoned casually for Thal and Hoddan to follow her.

"My chieftain," said Thal tremulously, "do we depart too?"

"Yes!" rasped Don Loris. "Get out of my sight!"

Thal moved with agility in the wake of the Lady Fani. Hoddan picked up his bag and followed. This, he considered darkly, was in the nature of a reprieve only; if those three spaceships overhead did come from Walden…but why three?

The Lady Fani went out the door she'd entered by. Some of the spearmen went ahead, and others closed in behind her. Hoddan followed. There were stone steps leading upward. They were steep and uneven and interminable. Hoddan climbed on aching legs for what seemed ages.

Stars appeared. The leading spearmen stepped out on a flag-stoned level area. When Hoddan got there he saw that they had arrived at the battlements of a high part of the castle wall. Starlight showed a rambling wall of circumvallation, with peaked roofs inside it. He could look down into a courtyard where a fire burned and several men busily did things beside it. But there were no other lights. Beyond the castle wall the ground stretched away toward a nearby range of rugged low mountains. It was vaguely splotched with different degrees of darkness, where fields and pastures and woodland copses stood.

"Here's a bench," said Fani cheerfully, "and you can sit down beside me and explain things. What's your name, again, and where did you come from?"

"I'm Bron Hoddan," said Hoddan. He found himself scowling. "I come from Zan, where everybody is a space-pirate. My grandfather heads the most notorious of the pirate gangs."

"Wonderful!" said Fani, admiringly. "I knew you couldn't be just an ordinary person and fight like my father said you did today!"

Thal cleared his throat.

"Lady Fani."

"Hush!" said Fani. "You're a nice old fuddy-duddy that father sent to the spaceport because he figured you'd be too timid to get into trouble. Hush!" To Hoddan she said, "Now, tell me all about the fighting. It must have been terrible!" She watched him with her head on one side, expectantly.

"The fighting I did today," said Hoddan angrily, "was exactly as dangerous and as difficult as shooting fish in a bucket. A little more trouble, but not much."

Even in the starlight he could see that her expression was more admiring than before.

"I thought you'd say something like that!" she said contentedly. "Go on!"

"That's all," said Hoddan.

"Quite all?"

"I can't think of anything else," he told her. He added drearily: "I rode a horse for three hours today. I'm not used to it. I ache. Your father is thinking of putting me in a dungeon until some scheme or other of his goes through. I'm disappointed. I'm worried about three lights that went across the sky at sundown and I'm simply too tired and befuddled for normal conversation."

"Oh," said Fani.

"If I may take my leave," said Hoddan querulously, "I'll get some rest and do some thinking when I get up. I'll hope to have more entertaining things to say."

He got to his feet and picked up his bag.

"Where do I go?" he asked.

Fani regarded him enigmatically. Thal squirmed.

"Thal will show you." Then Fani said deliberately, "Bron Hoddan, will you fight for me?"

Thal plucked anxiously at his arm. Hoddan said politely:

"If at all desirable, yes."

"Thank you," said Fani. "I am troubled by the Lord Ghek." She watched him move away. Thal, moaning softly, went with him down another monstrosity of a stone stairway.

"Oh, what folly!" mourned Thal. "I tried to warn you! You would not pay attention! When the Lady Fani asked if you would fight for her, you should have said if her father permitted you that honor. But you said yes! The spearmen heard you! Now you must either fight the Lord Ghek within a night and day or be disgraced!"

"I doubt," said Hoddan tiredly, "that the obligations of Darthian gentility apply to the grandson of a pirate or an escap—to me."

"But they do apply!" said Hoddan, shocked. "A man who has been disgraced has no rights! Any man may plunder him, any man may kill him at will. But if he resists plundering or kills anybody else in self-defense, he is hanged!"

Hoddan stopped short in his descent of the uneven stone steps.

"That's me from now on?" he asked sardonically. "Of course the Lady Fani didn't mean to put me on such a spot!"

"You were not polite," explained Thal. "She'd persuaded her father out of putting us in a dungeon until he thought of us again. You should at least have shown good manners! You should have said that you came here across deserts and flaming oceans because of the fame of her beauty. You might have said you heard songs of her sweetness beside campfires many worlds away. She might not have believed you, but—"

"Hold it!" said Hoddan. "That's, just manners? What do you say to a girl you really like?"

"Oh, then," said Thal, "you get complimentary!"

Hoddan went heavily down the rest of the steps. He was not in the least pleased. On a strange world, with strange customs, and with his weapons losing their charges every hour, he did not need any handicaps. But if he got into a worse-than-outlawed category such as Thal described...

At the bottom of the stairs he said, seething:

"When you've tucked me in bed, go back and ask the Lady Fani to arrange for me to have a horse and permission to go fight this Lord Ghek right after breakfast!"

He was too much enraged to think further. He let himself be led into some sort of quarters which probably answered Don Loris' description of a cozy dungeon. Thal vanished and came back with ointments for Hoddan's blisters, but no food. He explained again that if food were given to Hoddan would make it disgraceful to cut his throat. And Hoddan swore poisonously, but stripped off his garments and smeared himself lavishly where he had lost skin. The ointment stung like fire, and he presently lay awake in a sort of dreary fury. And he was ravenous.

It seemed to him that he lay awake for aeons, but he must have dozed off because he was wakened by a yell. It was not a complete yell, only the first part of one. It stopped in a particularly unpleasant fashion, and its echoes went reverberating through the stony walls of the castle. Hoddan was out of bed with a stun-pistol in his hand in a hurry. The first yell was followed by other shouts and outcries, by the clashing of steel upon steel, and all the frenzied tumult of combat in the dark. The uproar moved. In seconds the sound of fighting came from a plainly different direction, as if the striking force were rushing through only indifferently defended corridors.

It would not pass before Hoddan's door, but he growled to himself. On a feudal world, presumably one might expect anything. But there was a situation in being, here, in which etiquette required a rejected suitor to carry off a certain scornful maiden by force. Some young lordling named Ghek had to carry off Fani or be considered a man of no spirit.

A chemical gun went off somewhere. It went off again. There was almost an instant of silence. Then an intolerable screeching of triumph, and shrieks of another sort entirely, and the excessively loud clash of arms once more.

Hoddan was now clothed. He jerked on the door to open it.

The door was locked. He raged. He flung himself against it and it barely quivered. It was barred on the outside. He swore in highly indecorous terms, and tore his bedstead apart to get a battering-ram.

The fighting reached a climax. He heard a girl scream, and without question knew that it was Lady Fani, and equally without question knew that he would fight to keep any girl from being abducted by a man she didn't want to marry. He swung the log which was the corner-post of his bed. Something cracked. He swung again.

The sound of battle changed to that of a running fight. The objective of the raiders had been reached. Having gotten what they came for—and it could only be Fani—they retreated swiftly, fighting only to cover their retreat. Hoddan swung his bed-leg with furious anger. He heard a flurry of yells and swordplay, and a fierce, desperate cry from Fani among them, and a plank in his guestroom-dungeon-door gave way. He struck again. The running raiders poured past a corner some yards away. He battered and swore, and swore and battered as the tumult moved, and he suddenly heard a scurrying thunder of horses' hoofs outside the castle. There were yells of derisive triumph and the pounding, rumbling sound of horses headed away in the night.

Still raging inarticulately, Hoddan crashed his small log at the door. He was not consciously concerned about the distress Don Loris might feel over the abduction of his daughter. But there is an instinct in most men against the forcing of a girl to marriage against her will. Hoddan battered at his door. Around him the castle began to hum like a hive of bees. Women cried out or exclaimed, and men shouted furiously to one another; off-duty fighting men came belatedly, looking for somebody to fight, dragging weapons behind them and not knowing where to find enemies.

Bron Hoddan probably made as much noise as any four of them. Somebody brought a light somewhere near. It shone through the cracks in the splintered planks. He could see to aim. He smote savagely and the door came apart. It fell outward and he found himself in the corridor outside, being stared at by complete strangers.

"It's the engineer," someone explained to someone else. "I saw him when he rode in with Thal."

"I want Thal," said Hoddan coldly. "I want a dozen horses. I want men to ride them with me." He pushed his way forward. "Which way to the stables?"

But then he went back and picked up his bag of stun-pistols. His air was purposeful and his manner furious. The retainers of Don Loris were in an extremely apologetic frame of mind. The Lady Fani had been carried off into the night by a raiding-party undoubtedly led by Lord Ghek. The defenders of the castle hadn't prevented it. So there was no special reason to obey Hoddan, but there was every reason to seem to be doing something useful.

He found himself almost swept along by agitated retainers trying to look as if they were about a purposeful affair. They went down a long ramp, calling uneasily to each other. They eddied around a place where two men lay quite still on the floor. Then there were shouts of, "Thal! This way, Thal!" and Hoddan found himself in a small, stone-walled courtyard. It was filled with milling figures and many waving torches. And there was Thal, desperately pale and frightened. Behind him there was Don Loris, his eyes burning and his hands twitching, literally speechless from fury.

"Pick a dozen men, Thal!" commanded Hoddan. "Get 'em on horses! Get a horse for me, dammit! I'll show 'em how to use the stun-pistols as we ride!"

Thal panted, shaking:

"They hamstrung most of the horses!"

"Get the ones that are left!" barked Hoddan. He suddenly raged at Don Loris. "Here's another time stun-pistols get used on Darth! Object to this if you want to!"

Hoofbeats. Thal on a horse that shied and reared at the flames and confusion. Other horses, skittish and scared, with the smell of spilled blood in their nostrils, fighting the men who led them, their eyes rolling.

Thal called names as he looked about him. There was plenty of light. As he called a name, a man climbed on a horse. Some of the chosen men swaggered; some looked woefully unhappy. But with Don Loris glaring frenziedly upon them in the smoky glare, no man refused.

Hoddan climbed ungracefully upon the mount that four or five men held for him. Thal, with a fine sense of drama, seized a torch and waved it above his head. There was a vast creaking, and an unsuspected gate opened, and Thal rode out with a great clattering of hoofs and the others rode out after him.

There were lights everywhere about the castle, now. All along the battlements men had lighted the fire-baskets and lowered them partway down the walls, to disclose any attacking force which might have dishonorable intentions toward the stronghold. Others waved torches from the battlements. Streaming smoke, lighted by the flames, made weird patterns in the starlit night.

Thal swung his torch and pointed to the ground.

"They rode here!" he called to Hoddan. "They ride for Ghek's castle!"

Hoddan said angrily:

"Put out that light! Do you want to advertise how few we are and what were doing? Here, ride close!"

Thal flung down the torch. There was confusion and crowding on Hoddan's right-hand side. The smell of horseflesh was strong. Thal boomed:

"The pickings should be good, eh? Why do you want me?"

"You've got to learn something," snapped Hoddan. "Here! This is a stun-pistol. It's set for single-shot firing only. You hold it so, with your fingers along this rod. You point your finger at a man and pull this trigger. The pistol will buzz briefly. You let the trigger loose and point at another man and pull the trigger again. Understand? Don't try to use it over ten yards. You're no marksman! And don't waste charges! Remember what to do?"

There on a galloping horse beside Hoddan in the darkness, Thal zestfully repeated his lesson.

"Show another man and send him to me for a pistol." Hoddan commanded curtly. "I'll be showing others."

He turned to the man who rode too close to his left. Before he had fully instructed that man, another clamored for a weapon on his right. Hoddan checked his instructions and armed him.

The band of pursuing horsemen pounded through the dark night under strangely patterned stars. Hoddan held on to his saddle and barked out instructions to teach Darthians how to shoot.

He felt very queer. He began to worry. With the lights of Don Loris' castle long vanished behind, he began to realize how very small his troop of pursuers happened to be. They'd be outnumbered many times by those they sought to pursue.

Thal had said something about horses being hamstrung. There must, then, have been two attacking parties. One swarmed into the stables and drew all defending retainers there. Then the other poured over a wall or in through a bribed-open sally port, and rushed for the Lady Fani's apartments. The point was that the attackers had made sure there could be only a token pursuit. They knew they were many times stronger than any who might come after them. It would be absurd for them to flee.

Hoddan kicked his horse and got up to the front of the column of riders.

"Thal!" he snapped. "They'll be idiots if they keep on running away, now they're too far off to worry about men on foot. They'll stop and wait for us…most of them anyhow. We're riding into an ambush!"

"Good pickings, eh?" said Thal enthusiastically. "It would be disgrace not to fight them. The plunder—"

"Idiot!" yelped Hoddan. "These men know you. You know what I can do with stun-pistols! Tell them we're riding into ambush. They're to follow close behind us two! Tell them they're not to shoot at anybody more than five yards off and not coming at them, and if any man stops to plunder I'll kill him personally!"

Thal gaped at him.

"Not stop to plunder?"

"Ghek won't!" snapped Hoddan. "He'll take Fani on to his castle, leaving most of his men behind to massacre us! We've got to catch up to him before he shuts his castle gate in our faces!"

Thal reined aside and Hoddan pounded on at the head of the tiny troop. This was the second time in his life he'd been on a horse. He held on doggedly, riding with all the grace and spirit of a sack of cement. This adventure was not exhilarating. He was badly worried about innumerable things that could go wrong. Even if everything went right he'd still have plenty of troubles! It came into his mind, depressingly, that supposedly stirring action like this was really no more satisfying than piracy or the practice of electronics as a business. It was something one got into and had to go through with. Fani, for example, had tricked him into a fix in which he had to fight Ghek or be disgraced—and to be disgraced on Darth was equivalent to suicide.

His horse started up a gentle rise in the ground. It grew steeper. The horse slacked in its galloping. The incline grew steeper still. The horse slowed to a walk. Soon the dim outline of trees appeared overhead.

"Perfect place for an ambush," Hoddan reflected dourly.

He got out a stun-pistol. He set the stud for continuous fire—something he hadn't dared trust to the others.

His horse breasted the rise. There was a yell ahead and dim figures plunged toward him.

He painstakingly made ready to swing his stun-pistol from his extreme right all the way to the extreme left. The pistol should be capable of continuous fire for four seconds. But it was operating on stored charge. He didn't dare count on more than three.

He pulled the trigger. The stun-pistol hummed; its noise was inaudible through the yells of the charging partisans of the Lord Ghek.

# CHAPTER V

Hoddan swore from the depths of a very considerable vocabulary.

"You—get back on your horses, or I'll blast you and leave you for Ghek's men to handle when they're able to move about again! Get back on those horses!"

The men got back on their horses.

"Now go on ahead," rasped Hoddan. "All of you! I'm going to count you!"

The dozen horsemen from Don Loris' stronghold rode reluctantly on ahead. He did count them. He rode on, shepherding them before him.

"Ghek," he told them in a blood-curdling tone, "has a bigger prize than any cash you'll plunder from one of his shot-down retainers! He's got the Lady Fani! He won't stop before he has her behind castle walls! We've got to catch up with him! Do you want to try to climb into his castle by your fingernails? You'll do it if he gets there first!"

The horses moved a little faster. Thal said with surprising humility:

"If we force our horses too much, they'll be exhausted before we can catch up."

"Figure it out," snapped Hoddan. "We have to catch up!"

He settled down to more of the acute discomfort that riding was to him. Hoddan knew that his party was slowed down by him. Presently he began to feel bitterly sure that Ghek would reach his castle before he was overtaken.

"This place he's heading for," he said discouragedly to Thal, "any chance of our rushing it?"

"Oh, no!" said Thal dolefully. "Ten men could hold it against a thousand!"

"Then can't we make better time?"

Thal said resignedly:

"Ghek probably had fresh horses waiting, so he could keep on at top speed in his flight. I doubt that we will catch him, now."

"The Lady Fani," said Hoddan bitterly, "has put me in a fix so if I don't fight him I'm ruined!"

"Disgraced," corrected Thal. He added mournfully, "It's the same thing."

Gloom descended on the whole party as it filled their leaders. Insensibly, the pace of the horses slackened still more. They had done well. But a horse that can cover fifty miles a day at its own gait, can be exhausted in ten or less, if pushed. By the time Hoddan and his men were within two miles of Ghek's castle, their mounts were extremely reluctant to move faster than a walk. At a mile, they were kept in motion only by kicks.

The route they followed was specific. There was no choice of routes, here in the hills. They could only follow every twist and turn of the trail, among steep mountain flanks and minor peaks. But suddenly they came to a clear, wide valley; yellow cressets burned at its upper end, no more than a half mile distant. They showed a castle gate, open, with the last of a party of horsemen filing into it. Even as Hoddan swore, the gate closed. Faint shouts of triumph came from inside the castle walls.

"I'd have bet on this," said Hoddan miserably. "Stop here, Thal. Pick out a couple of your more hangdog characters and fix them up with their hands apparently tied behind their backs. We take a breather for five minutes."

He would not let any man dismount. He shifted himself about on his own saddle, trying to find a comfortable way to sit. He failed. At the end of five minutes he gave orders. There were still shouts occasionally from within Ghek's castle. They had that unrhythmic frequency which suggested that they were responses to a speech. Ghek was making a fine, dramatic spectacle of his capture of an unwilling bride. He was addressing his retainers and saying that through their fine loyalty, co-operation and willingness to risk all for their chieftain, they now had the Lady Fani to be their chatelaine. He thanked them from the bottom of his heart and they were invited to the official wedding, which would take place some time tomorrow, most likely.

Before the speech was quite finished, however, Hoddan and his weary followers rode up into the patch of light cast by the cressets outside the walls. Thal bellowed to the battlements.

"Prisoners!" he roared, according to instructions from Hoddan. "We caught some prisoners in the ambush! They got fancy news! Tell Lord Ghek he'd better get their story right off! No time to waste! Urgent!"

Hoddan played the part of one prisoner, just in case anybody noticed from above that one man rode as if either entirely unskilled in riding or else injured in a fight.

He heard shoutings, over the walls. He glared at his men and they drooped in their saddles. The gate creaked open and the horsemen from Don Loris' castle filed inside. They showed no elation, because Hoddan had promised to ram a spear down the throat of any man who gave away his strategy ahead of time. The gate closed behind them. Men came to take their horses. This could have revealed that the newcomers were strangers, but Ghek would have recruited new and extra retainers for the emergency of tonight. There would be many strange faces in his castle just now.

"Good fight, eh?" bellowed an ancient, long-retired retainer with a wine bottle in his hand.

"Good fight," agreed Thal.

"Good plunder, eh?" bellowed the ancient above the heads of younger men. "Like the good old days?"

"Better!" boomed Thal.

At just this instant the young Lord Ghek's personal servant appeared.

"What's this about prisoners with fancy news?" he demanded. "What is it?"

"Don Loris!" whooped Thal. "Long live the Lady Fani!"

Hoddan carefully opened fire with the continuous-fire stud of this pistol—his third tonight—pressed down. The merrymakers in the courtyard wavered and went down in windrows. Thal opened fire with a stun-pistol. The others bellowed and began to fling bolts at every living thing they saw.

"To the Lady Fani!" rasped Hoddan, getting off his horse with as many creakings as the castle gate.

His followers now dismounted. They fired with reckless abandon. A stun-pistol, which does not kill, imposes few restraints upon its user. If you shoot somebody who doesn't need to be shot, he may not like it but he isn't permanently harmed. So the twelve who'd followed Hoddan poured in what would have been a murderous fire if they'd been shooting bullets, but was no worse than devastating as matters stood.

There were screams and flight and utterly hopeless defiances by sword-armed and spear-armed men. In instants Hoddan went limping into the castle with Thal by his side, searching for Fani and Lord Ghek. Hoddan's men went raging happily through corridors and halls. They used their stun-pistols with zest. Hoddan heard Fani scream angrily and he and Thal went swiftly to see. They came upon the young Lord Ghek trying to let Fani down out of a window on a rope. He undoubtedly intended to follow her and complete his abduction on the run. But Fani bit him, and Hoddan said vexedly:

"Look here! It seems that I'm disgraced if I don't fight you somehow—"

The young Lord Ghek rushed him, sword out, eyes blazing in a fine frenzy of despair. Hoddan brought him down with a buzz of the stun-gun.

One of Hoddan's followers came hunting for him.

"Sir," he sputtered, "we got the garrison cornered in their quarters, and we've been picking them off through the windows, and they think they're dropping dead and want to surrender. Shall we let 'em?"

"By all means," Hoddan said irritably. "And Thal, go get something heavier than a nightgown for the Lady Fani to wear, and then do what plundering is practical. But I want to be out of here in a half-hour. Understand?"

"I'll attend to the costume," said the Lady Fani vengefully. "You cut his throat while I'm getting dressed."

She nodded at the unconscious Lord Ghek on the pavement. She disappeared through a door nearby. Hoddan could guess that Ghek would have prepared something elaborate in the way of a trousseau for the bride he was to carry screaming from her home. Somehow it was the sort of thing a Darthian would do. Now Fani would enjoyably attire herself in the best of it.

"Thal," said Hoddan, "help me get this character into a closet somewhere. He's not to be killed. I don't like him, but at this moment I don't like anybody very much, and I won't play favorites."

Thal dragged the insensible young nobleman into the next room. Hoddan locked the door and pocketed the key as Fani came into view again. She was splendidly attired, now, in brocade and jewels. Ghek had evidently hoped to placate her after marriage by things of that sort and had spent lavishly for them.

Now, throughout the castle there were many and diverse noises. Sometimes—not often—there was still the crackling hum of a stun-pistol. There were many more exuberant shoutings. They apparently had to do with loot. There were some squealings in female voices, but many more gigglings.

"I need not say," said the Lady Fani with dignity, "that I thank you very much. But I do say so."

"You're quite welcome," said Hoddan politely.

"And what are you going to do now?"

"I imagine," said Hoddan, "that we'll go down into the courtyard where our horses are. I gave my men a half-hour to loot in. During that half-hour I shall sit down on something which will, I hope, remain perfectly still. And I may," he added morbidly, "I may eat an apple. I've had nothing to eat since I landed on Darth. People don't want to commit themselves to not cutting my throat. But after one half-hour we'll leave."

The Lady Fani looked sympathetic.

"But the castle's surrendered to you," she protested. "You hold it! Aren't you going to try to keep it?"

"There are a good many unpleasant characters out yonder," said Hoddan, waving his hand at the great outdoors, "who've reason to dislike me very much. They'll be anxious to express their emotions, when they feel up to it. I want to dodge them. And presently the people in this castle will realize that even stun-pistols can't keep on shooting indefinitely here. I don't want to be around when it occurs to them."

He offered his arm with a reasonably grand air and went limping with her down to the courtyard just inside the gate. Two of Don Loris' retainers staggered into view as they arrived, piling up plunder which ranged from a quarter-keg of wine to a mass of frothy stuff which must be female garments. They went away and other men arrived loaded down their own accumulations of loot. Some of the local inhabitants looked on with uneasy indignation.

Hoddan found a bench and sat down. He conspicuously displayed one of the weapons which had captured the castle. Ghek s defeated retainers looked at him darkly.

"Bring me something to eat," commanded Hoddan. "Then if you bring fresh horses for my men, and one extra for each to carry his plunder on, I'll take them away. I'll even throw in the Lord Ghek, who is now unharmed, but with his life in the balance. Otherwise—"

He moved the pistol suggestively. The normal inhabitants of Ghek's castle moved away, discussing the situation in subdued voices.

The Lady Fani sat down proudly on the bench beside him.

"You are wonderful!" she said with conviction.

"I used to cherish that illusion myself," said Hoddan.

"But nobody before in all Darthian history has ever fought twenty men, and then thirty men, and destroyed an ambush, and captured a castle, all in one day!"

"And without a meal," said Hoddan darkly, "and with a lot of blisters."

He considered. Somebody came running with bread and cheese and wine. He bit into the bread and cheese. After a moment he said, his mouth full:

"I once saw a man perform the unparalleled feat of jumping over nine barrels placed in a row. It had never been done before. But I didn't envy him. I never wanted to jump over nine barrels in a row! In the same way, I never especially wanted to fight other men or break up ambushes or capture castles. I want to do what I want to do, not what other people happen to admire."

"Then what do you want to do?" she asked admiringly.

"I'm not sure now," said Hoddan gloomily. He took a fresh bite. "But a little while ago I wanted to do some interesting and useful things in electronics, and get reasonably rich, and marry a delightful girl, and become a prominent citizen on Walden. I think I'll settle for another planet, now."

"My father will make you rich," said the girl proudly. "You saved me from being married to Ghek!"

Hoddan shook his head.

"I've got my doubts," he said. "He had a scheme to import a lot of stun-pistols and arm his retainers with them. Then he meant to rush the spaceport and have me set up a broadcast power unit that'd keep them charged all the time. Then he'd sit back and enjoy life. Holding the spaceport, nobody else could get stun-weapons, and nobody could resist his retainers who had 'em. So he'd be top man on Darth. He'd have exactly as much power as he chose to seize. I think he cherished that little idea; but now I've given advance publicity to stun-pistols. Now he hasn't a ghost of a chance of pulling it off. I'm afraid he'll be displeased with me."

"I can take care of that!" said Fani confidently. She did not question that her father would be displeased.

"Maybe you can," said Hoddan, "but though he's kept a daughter he's lost a dream. And that's bereavement! I know!"

Horses came plodding into the courtyard with Ghek's retainers driving them. They were anxious to get rid of their conquerors. Hoddan's men came trickling back, with armfuls of plunder to add to the piles they'd previously gathered. Thal took charge, commanding the exchange of saddles from tired to fresh horses and that the booty be packed on the extra mounts. It was time. Nine of the dozen looters were at work on the task when there was a tumult back in the castle. Yellings and the clash of steel. Hoddan shook his head.

He conjectured that somebody's pistol went empty and the local boys found it out.

He beckoned to a listening, tense, resentful inhabitant of the castle. He held up the key of the room in which he'd locked young Ghek.

"Now open the castle gate," he commanded, "and fetch out my last three men, and we'll leave without setting fire to anything. The Lord Ghek would like it that way. He's locked up in a room that's particularly inflammable."

The last statement was a guess, only, but Ghek's retainer looked horrified. He bellowed. There was a subtle change in the bitterly hostile atmosphere. Men came angrily to help load the spare horses. Hoddan's last three men came out of a corridor, wiping blood from various scratches and complaining plaintively that their pistols had shot empty and they'd had to defend themselves with knives.

Three minutes later the cavalcade rode out of the castle gate and away into the darkness. Hoddan had arrived here when Ghek was inside with Fani as his prisoner, when there were only a dozen men without and at least a hundred inside to defend the walls. And the castle was considered impregnable.

In a half-hour Hoddan's followers had taken the castle, rescued Fani, looted it superficially, gotten fresh horses for themselves and spare ones for their plunder, and were headed away again. In only one respect were they worse off than when they arrived. Some stun-pistols were empty.

Hoddan searched the sky and pieced together the star pattern he'd noted before.

"Hold it!" he said sharply to Thal. "We don't go back the same way we came! The gang that ambushed us will be stirring around again, and we haven't got full stun-pistols now! We make a wide circle around those characters!"

"Why?" demanded Thal. "There are only so many passes. The only other one is three times as long. And it is disgraceful to avoid a fight."

"Thal!" snapped an icy voice from beside Hoddan. "You have an order! Obey it!"

Even in the darkness, Hoddan could see Thal jump.

"Yes, my Lady Fani," said Thal shakily. "But we go a long distance roundabout."

The direction of motion through the night now changed. The long line of horses moved in deepest darkness, lessened only by the light of many stars. Even so, in time one's eyes grew accustomed and it was a glamorous spectacle.

Presently they came to a narrow defile which opened out before them. And there, far, far away, they could see the sky as vaguely brighter. As they went on, indeed, a glory of red and golden colorings appeared at the horizon.

And out of that magnificence three bright lights suddenly darted. In strict V-formation, they flashed from the sunrise toward the west. They went overhead, more brilliant than the brightest stars, and when partway down to the horizon they suddenly winked out.

"What on Earth are they?" demanded Fani. "I never saw anything like that before!"

"They're spaceships in orbit," said Hoddan. He was as astounded as the girl, but for a different reason. "I thought they'd be landed by now!"

It changed everything. He could not see what the change amounted to, but the change was there.

"We're going to the spaceport," he told Thal curtly. "We'll recharge our stun-pistols there. I thought those ships had landed. They haven't. Now we'll see if we can keep them aloft! How far to the landing-grid?"

"You insisted," complained Thal, "that we not go back to Don Loris' castle by the way we left it. There are only so many passes through the hills. The only other one is very long. We are only four miles—"

"Then we head there right now!" snapped Hoddan. "And we step up the speed!"

He barked commands to his followers. Thal, puzzled but in dread of acid comment from Fani, bustled up and down the line of men, insisting on a faster pace. Finally even the led horses, loaded with loot, managed to get up to a respectable ambling trot. The sunrise proceeded. Dew upon the straggly grass became visible. Separate drops appeared as gems upon the grass blades, and then began gradually to vanish as the sun's disk showed itself. Then the angular metal framework of the landing-grid rose dark against the sunrise sky.

When they rode up to it, Hoddan reflected that it was the only really civilized structure on the planet. Architecturally it was surely the least pleasing. It had been built when Darth was first settled on, and when ideas of commerce and interstellar trade seemed reasonable. It was a half-mile high and built of massive metal beams. It loomed hugely overhead when the double file of shaggy horses trotted under its lower arches and across the grass-grown space within it. Hoddan headed purposefully for the control shed. There was no sign of movement anywhere. The steeply gabled roofs of the nearby town showed only the fluttering of tiny birds. No smoke rose from chimneys. Yet the slanting morning sunshine was bright.

As Hoddan actually reached the control shed, he saw a sleepy man in the act of putting a key in the door. He dismounted within feet of that man, who turned and blinked sleepily at him, and then immediately looked the reverse of cordial. It was the same man he'd stung with a stun-pistol the day before.

"I've come back," said Hoddan, "for a few more kilowatts.

The red-headed man swore angrily.

"Hush!" said Hoddan gently. "The Lady Fani is with us." The red-headed man jerked his head around and paled. Thal glowered at him. Others of Don Loris' retainers shifted their positions significantly, to make their oversized knives handier.

"We'll come in," said Hoddan. "Thal, collect the pistols and bring them inside."

Fani swung lightly to the ground and followed him in. She looked curiously at the cables and instrument boards and switches inside. On one wall a red light pulsed, and went out, and pulsed again. The red-headed man looked at it.

"You're being called," said Hoddan. "Don't answer it."

The red-headed man scowled. Thal came in with an armful of stun-pistols in various stages of discharge. Hoddan briskly broke the butt of one of his own and presented it to the terminals he'd used the day before.

"He's not to touch anything, Thal," said Hoddan. To the red-headed man he observed, "I suspect that call's been coming in all night. Something was in orbit at sundown. You closed up shop and went home early, eh?"

"Why not?" rasped the red-headed man. "There's only one ship a month!"

"Sometimes," said Hoddan, "there are specials. But I commend your negligence. It was probably good for me."

He charged one pistol, and snapped its butt shut, and snapped open another, and charged it. There was no difficulty, of course. In minutes all the pistols he'd brought from Walden were ready for use again.

He tucked away as many as he could conveniently carry on his person. He handed the rest to Thal. He went competently to the pulsing red signal. He put headphones to his ears. He listened. His expression became extremely strange, as if he did not quite understand nor wholly believe what he heard.

"Odd," he said mildly. He considered for a moment or two. Then he rummaged around in the drawers of desks. He found wire clippers. He began to snip wires in half.

The red-headed man started forward automatically. "Take care of him, Thal," said Hoddan.

He cut the microwave receiver free of its wires and cables. He lifted it experimentally and opened part of its case to make sure the thermo battery that would power it in an emergency was there and in working order. It was.

"Put this on a horse, Thal," commanded Hoddan. "We're taking it up to Don Loris'."

The red-headed man's mouth dropped open. He said stridently:

"Hey! You can't do that!" Hoddan glared at him. The redhead then said sourly: "All right, you can. I'm not trying to stop you with all those hardcases outside!"

"You can build another in a week," said Hoddan kindly. "You must have spare parts."

Thal carried the communicator outside. Hoddan opened a cabinet, threw switches, and painstakingly cut and snipped and snipped at a tangle of wires within.

"Just your instrumentation," he explained. "You won't use the grid until you've got this fixed, too. A few days of harder work than you're used to. That's all!"

He led the way out again, and on the way explained to Fani:

"Pretty old-fashioned job, this grid. They make simpler ones nowadays. They'll be able to repair it, though, in time. Now we go back to your father's castle. He may not be pleased, but he should be mollified."

He saw Fani mount lightly into her own saddle and shook his head gloomily. He climbed clumsily into his own. They moved off to return to Don Loris' stronghold. Hoddan suffered.

They reached the castle before noon, and the sight of the Lady Fani produced enthusiasm and loud cheers. The loot displayed by the returned wayfarers increased the rejoicing. There was envy among the men who had stayed behind. There were respectfully admiring looks cast upon Hoddan. He had displayed, in furnishing opportunities for plunder, the most-admired quality a leader of feudal fighting men could show.

The Lady Fani beamed as she, Thal, and Hoddan, all very dusty and travel-stained, presented themselves to her father in the castle's great hall.

"Here's your daughter, sir," said Hoddan, and yawned. "I hope there won't be any further trouble with Ghek. We took his castle and looted it a little and brought back some extra horses. Then we went to the spaceport. I recharged my stun-pistols and put the landing-grid out of order for the time being. I brought away the communicator there." He yawned again. "There's something highly improper going on, up just beyond atmosphere. There are three ships up there in orbit, and they were trying to call the spaceport in non-regulation fashion, and it's possible that some of your neighbors would be interested. So I postponed everything until I could get some sleep. It seemed to me that when better skullduggeries are concocted, that Don Loris and his associates ought to concoct them. And if you'll excuse me—"

He moved away practically dead on his feet. If he had been accustomed to horseback riding, he wouldn't have been so exhausted. But now he yawned, and yawned, and Thal took him to a room quite different from the guestroom-dungeon to which he'd been taken the night before. He noted that the door, this time, opened inward. He braced chairs against it to make sure that nobody could open it from without. He lay down and slept heavily.

He was awakened by loud poundings. He roused himself enough to say sleepily:

"Whaddyawant?"

"The lights in the sky!" cried Fani outside the door. "The ones you say are spaceships! It's sunset again, and I just saw them. But there aren't three, anymore. Now there are nine!"

"All right," said Hoddan. He lay down his head again and thrust it into his pillow. Then he was suddenly very wide awake. He sat up with a start.

Nine spaceships? That wasn't possible! That would be a spacefleet! And there were no spacefleets! Walden would certainly have never sent more than one ship to demand his surrender to its police. The Space Patrol never needed more than one ship anywhere. Commerce wouldn't cause ships to travel in company. *Piracy?* There couldn't be a pirate fleet! There'd never be enough loot anywhere to keep it in operation. Nine spaceships at one time. All traveling in orbit around a primitive planet like Darth.

It couldn't happen! Hoddan couldn't conceive of such a thing. But a recently developed pessimism suggested that since everything else, to date, had been to his disadvantage, this was probably a catastrophe also.

He groaned and lay down to sleep again.

# CHAPTER VI

When frantic bangings on the propped-shut door awakened him next morning, he confusedly imagined that they were noises in the communicator headphones. But suddenly he opened his eyes. Somebody banged on the door once more. A voice cried angrily:

"Bron Hoddan! Wake up or I'll go away and let whatever happens to you, happen! Wake up!"

It was the voice of the Lady Fani, at once indignant, tearful, solicitous and angry.

"Hello. I'm awake. What's up?"

"Come out of there!" cried Fani's voice, simultaneously exasperated and filled with anxiety. "Things are happening! Somebody's here from Walden! They want you!"

Hoddan could not believe it. It was too unlikely. But he opened the door and Thal came in, and Fani followed.

"Good morning," said Hoddan automatically.

Thal said mournfully:

"A *bad* morning, Bron Hoddan! A bad morning! Men from Walden came riding over the hills."

"How many?"

"Two," said Fani angrily. "A fat man in a uniform, and a young man who looks like he wants to cry. They had an escort of retainers from one of my father's neighbors. They were stopped at the gate, of course, and they sent a written message to my father, and he had them brought inside right away!"

Hoddan shook his head.

"They probably said that I'm a criminal and that I should be sent back to Walden. How'd they get down? The landing-grid isn't working."

"They landed in something that used rockets," Fani said viciously. "It came down close to a castle over that way—only six or seven miles from the spaceport. They asked for you. They said you'd landed from the last liner from Walden. And because you and Thal fought so splendidly, why everybody's talking about you. So the chieftain over there accepted a present of money from them, and gave them horses as a return gift, and sent them here with a guard. Thal talked to the guards. The men from Walden have promised huge gifts of money if they help take you back to the thing that uses rockets."

"I suspect," said Hoddan, "that it would be a spaceboat. Yes. With a built-in, tool-steel cell to keep me from telling anybody how to make—" He stopped and grimaced. "They'd take me to the spaceport in a soundproof can and I'd be hauled back to Walden. Fine!"

"What are you going to do?" asked Fani anxiously.

Hoddan's ideas were not clear. But Darth was not a healthy place for him. It was extremely likely, for example, that Don Loris would feel that the very bad jolt he'd given that astute schemer's plans, by using stun-pistols at the spaceport, had been neatly cancelled out by his rescue of Fani. He would regard Hoddan with a mingled gratitude and aversion that would amount to calm detachment. Don Loris could not be counted on as a really warm, personal friend.

On the other hand, the social system of Darth was not favorable to a stranger with an already lurid reputation for fighting. Another disadvantage was that his weapons would be useless unless frequently recharged; he couldn't count on always being able to do that.

As a practical matter, his best bet was probably to investigate the nine inexplicable ships overhead. They hadn't co-operated with the Waldenians. It could be inferred that no confidential relationship existed up there. It was even possible that the nine ships and the Waldenians didn't know of each other's presence. There is a lot of room in space. If both called on ship-frequency and listened on ground-frequency, they would not have picked up each others' summons to the ground.

"You've got to do something!" insisted Fani. "I saw father talking to them! He looked happy, and he never looks happy unless he's planning some skullduggery!"

"I think," said Hoddan, "that I'll have some breakfast, if I may. As soon as I fasten up my ship bag."

Thal said mournfully:

"If anything happens to you, something will happen to me too, because I helped you."

"Breakfast first," said Hoddan. "That, as I understand it, should make it disgraceful for your father to have my throat cut. But beyond that…" He said gloomily, "Thal, get a couple of horses outside the wall. We may need to ride somewhere. I'm very much afraid we will. But first I'd like to have some breakfast."

"But aren't you going to face them? You could shoot them!" Fani said.

Hoddan shook his head.

"It wouldn't solve anything. Anyhow a practical man like your father won't sell me out before he's sure I can't pay off better. I'll bet on a conference with me before he makes a deal."

Fani stamped her foot.

"Outrageous! Think what you saved me from!"

But she did not question the possibility. Hoddan observed.

"A practical man can always make what he wants to do look like a noble sacrifice of personal inclinations to the welfare of the community." Hoddan commented. "Now I've decided that I've got to be practical myself, and that's one of the rules. How about breakfast?"

He strapped the ship bag shut on the stun-pistols his pockets would not hold. He made a minor adjustment to the communicator. It was not ruined, but nobody else could use it without much labor finding out what he'd done. This was the sort of thing his grandfather on Zan would have advised. His grandfather's views were explicit.

"Helping one's neighbor," the old man had said frequently, "is all right as a two-way job. But maybe he's laying for you. You get a chance to fix him so he can't do you no harm and you're a lot better off and he's one hell of a better neighbor!"

This was definitely true of the men from Walden. Hoddan guessed that Derec was one of them. The other would represent the police or the planetary government. It was probably just as true of Don Loris and others.

Hoddan found himself disapproving of the way the cosmos was designed.

As he sat at breakfast, Fani looked at him with interesting anxiety; he was filled with forebodings. The future looked dark. Yet what he asked of fate and chance was so simple! He asked only a career, riches, and a delightful girl to marry and the admiration of his fellow citizens. Trivial things! But it looked like he'd have to do battle for even such minor gifts of destiny!

Fani watched him eat.

"I don't understand you," she complained. "Anybody else would be proud of what he'd done and angry with my father. Or don't you think he'll act ungratefully?"

"Of course I do!" said Hoddan.

"Then why aren't you angry?"

"I'm hungry," said Hoddan.

"And you take it for granted that I want to be properly grateful," said Fani in one breath, "and yet you haven't shown the least appreciation of my getting two horses over in that patch of woodland yonder!" she pointed and Hoddan nodded. "Besides having Thal there with orders to serve you faithfully—"

She stopped short. Don Loris appeared, beaming, at the top of the steps leading from the great hall where the conferences took place. He regarded Hoddan benignly.

"This is a very bad business, my dear fellow," he said benevolently. "Has Fani told you of the people who arrived from Walden in search of you? They tell me terrible things about you!"

"Yes," said Hoddan. He prepared a roll for biting. He continued, "One of them, I think, is named Derec. He's to identify me so good money isn't wasted paying for the wrong man. The other man's a policeman, isn't he?" He reflected a moment. "If I were you, I'd start talking at a million credits. You might get half that."

He bit into the roll as Don Loris looked shocked.

"Do you think," he asked indignantly," that I would give up the rescuer of my daughter to emissaries from a foreign planet, to be locked in a dungeon for life?"

"Not in those words," conceded Hoddan. "But after all, despite your deep gratitude to me, there are such things as one's duty to humanity as a whole. And while it would cause you bitter anguish if someone dear to you represented a danger to millions of innocent women and children—still, under such circumstances you might feel it necessary to do violence to your own emotions."

Don Loris looked at him with abrupt suspicion. Hoddan waved the roll.

"Moreover," he observed, "gratitude for actions done on Darth does not entitle you to be judge of my actions on Walden. While you might and even should feel obliged to defend me in all things I have done on Darth, your obligation to me does not extend to uphold my acts on Walden."

Don Loris looked extremely uneasy.

"I may have thought something like that," he admitted. "But—"

"So that," continued Hoddan, "while your debt to me cannot and should not be overlooked, nevertheless—" Hoddan put the roll into his mouth and spoke less clearly "—nevertheless you feel that you should give consideration to the claims of Walden to inquire into my actions while there."

He chewed, swallowed, and said gravely:

"And can I make death rays?"

Don Loris brightened. He drew a deep breath of relief. He said complainingly:

"I don't see why you're so sarcastic! Yes. That is a rather important question. You see, on Walden they don't know how to. They say you do. They're very anxious that nobody should be able to. Because, while in unscrupulous hands such an instrument of destruction would be most unfortunate... Ah...under proper control..."

"*Your,*" said Hoddan.

"Say *ours,*" said Don Loris hopefully. "With my experience of men and affairs, and my loyal and devoted retainers—"

"And cozy dungeons," said Hoddan. He wiped his mouth. "No."

Don Loris started violently.

"No, what?"

"No death rays," said Hoddan. "I can't make 'em. Nobody can. If they could be made, some star somewhere would be turning them out, or some natural phenomenon would let them loose from time to time. If there were such things as death rays, all living things would have died, or else would have adjusted to their weaker manifestations and developed immunity so they wouldn't be death days any longer. As a matter of fact, that's probably been the case, some time in the past. So far as the gadget goes that they're talking about, it's been in use for a half-century in the Cetis cluster. Nobody's died of it yet."

Don Loris looked bitterly disappointed.

"That's the truth?" he asked unhappily. "Honestly? That's your last word on it?"

"Much," said Hoddan, "much as I hate to spoil the prospects of profitable skullduggery, that's my last word and it's true."

"But those men from Walden are very anxious!" protested Don Loris. "There was no ship available, so their government got a liner that normally wouldn't stop here to take an extra lifeboat aboard. It came out of overdrive in this solar system, let out the lifeboat, and went on its way again. Those two men are extremely anxious!"

"Ambitious, maybe," said Hoddan. "They're prepared to pay to overcome your sense of gratitude to me. Naturally, you want all the traffic will bear. I think you can get a half-million."

Don Loris looked suspicious again.

"You don't seem worried," he said fretfully. "I don't understand you!"

"I have a secret," said Hoddan.

"What is it?"

"It will develop," said Hoddan.

Don Loris hesitated, and essayed to speak, and thought better of it. He shrugged his shoulders and went slowly back to the flight of stone steps. He descended. The Lady Fani started to wring her hands. Then she said hopefully:

"What's your secret?"

"That your father thinks I have one," said Hoddan. "Thanks for the breakfast. Should I walk out the gate, or—"

"It's closed," said the Lady Fani forlornly. "But I have a rope for you. You can go down over the wall."

"Thanks," said Hoddan. "It's been a pleasure to rescue you."

"Will you…" Fani hesitated. "I've never known anybody like you before. Will you ever come back?"

Hoddan shook his head at her.

"Once you asked me if I'd fight for you, and look what it got me into! No commitments."

He glanced along the battlements. There was a fairly large coil of rope in view. He picked up his bag and went over to it. He checked the fastening of one end and tumbled the other over the wall.

Ten minutes later he trudged up to Thal, waiting in the nearby woodland with two horses.

"The Lady Fani," he said "has the kind of brains I like. She pulled up the rope again."

Thal did not comment. He watched morosely as Hoddan made the perpetually present ship bag fast to his saddle and then distastefully climbed aboard the horse.

"What are you going to do?" asked Thal unhappily. "I didn't make a parting-present to Don Loris, so I'll be disgraced if he finds out I helped you. And I don't know where to take you."

"Where," asked Hoddan, "did those characters from Walden come down?"

Thal told him. At the castle of a powerful feudal chieftain, on the plain, some four miles from the mountain range, and six miles this side of the spaceport.

"We ride there," said Hoddan. "Liberty is said to be sweet, but the man who said that didn't have blisters from a saddle. Let's go."

They rode away. There would be no immediate pursuit, and possibly none at all. Don Loris had left Hoddan at breakfast on the battlements. The Lady Fani would make as much confusion over his disappearance as she could. But there'd be no search for him until Don Loris had made his deal.

Hoddan was sure that Fani's father would have an enjoyable morning. He would relish the bargaining session. He'd explain in great detail how valuable had been Hoddan's service to him, in rescuing Fani from an abductor who would have been an intolerable son-in-law. He'd grow almost tearful as he described his affection for Hoddan, and how he loved his daughter. He would observe aggrievedly that they were asking him to betray the man who had saved for him the solace of his old age. He would mention also that the price they offered was an affront to his paternal affection and his dignity. Either they'd come up or the deal was off!

But meanwhile Hoddan and Thal rode industriously toward the place from which those emissaries had come.

All was tranquil. All was calm. Once they saw a dust cloud, and Thal turned aside to a providential wooded copse, in which they remained while a cavalcade went by. Thal explained that it was a feudal chieftain on his way to the spaceport town. It was simple discretion for them not to be observed, said Thal, because they had great reputations as fighting men. Whoever defeated them would become prominent at once. So somebody might try to pick a quarrel under one of the finer points of etiquette when it would be disgrace to use anything but standard Darthian implements for massacre. Hoddan admitted that he did not feel quarrelsome.

They rode on after a time, and in late afternoon the towers and battlements of the castle they sought appeared. The ground here was only gently rolling. They approached it with caution, following the reverse slope of hills. At last they penetrated horse-high brush to the point where they could see it clearly.

If Hoddan had been a student of early terrestrial history, he might have remarked upon the re-emergence of ancient architectural forms to match the revival of primitive social systems. As it was, he noted in this feudal castle the use of bastions for flanking fire upon attackers; he recognized the value of battlements for the protection of defenders while allowing them to shoot, and the tricky positioning of sally ports. He even grasped the reason for the massive, stark, unornamented keep. But his eyes did not stay on the castle for long. He saw the spaceboat in which Derec and his more authoritative companion had arrived.

It lay on the ground a half-mile from the castle walls. It was a chubby, clumsy, flattened shape some forty feet long and nearly fifteen wide. The ground about it was scorched where it had descended upon its rocket flames. There were several horses tethered near it, and men who were plainly retainers of the nearby castle reposed in its shade.

Hoddan reined in.

"Here we part," he told Thal. "When we first met I enabled you to pick the pockets of a good many of your fellow countrymen. I never asked for my split of the take. I expect you to remember me with affection."

Thal clasped both of Hoddan's hands in his.

"If you ever return," he said with mournful warmth, "I am your friend!"

Hoddan nodded and rode out of the brushwood toward the spaceboat lifeboat that had landed the emissaries from Walden. That it landed so close to the spaceport, of course, was no accident. It was known on Walden that Hoddan had taken space-passage to Darth. He'd have landed only two days before his pursuers could reach the planet. And on a roadless, primitive world like Darth he couldn't have gotten far from the spaceport. So his pursuers would have landed close by, also. But it must have taken considerable courage. When the landing-grid failed to answer, it must have seemed likely that Hoddan's death rays had been at work.

Here and now, though, there was no uneasiness. Hoddan rode heavily, without haste, through the slanting sunshine. He was seen from a distance and watched without apprehension by the loafing guards about the boat. He looked hot and thirsty. He was both. So the posted guard merely looked at him without too much interest when he brought his dusty mount up to the shadow the lifeboat cast, and apparently decided that there wasn't room to get into it.

He grunted a greeting and looked at them speculatively.

"Those two characters from Walden," he observed, "sent me to get something from this thing, here. Don Loris told 'em I was a very honest man."

He painstakingly looked like a very honest man. After a moment there were responsive grins.

"If there's anything missing when I start back," said Hoddan, "I can't imagine how it happened! None of you would take anything. Oh, no! I bet you'll blame it on me!" He shook his head and said, "Tsk. Tsk. Tsk."

One of the guards sat up and said appreciatively:

"But it's locked. Good."

"Being an honest man," said Hoddan amiably, "they told me how to unlock it."

He got off his horse. He removed the bag from his saddle. He went into the grateful shadow of the metal hull. He paused and mopped his face and then went to the boat's port. He put his hand on the turning-bar. Then he painstakingly pushed in the locking-stud with his other hand. Of course the handle turned. The port opened. The two from Walden would have thought everything safe because it was under guard. On Walden that protection would have been enough. On Darth, the spaceboat had not been looted simply because locks, there, were not made with separate vibration-checks to keep vibration from loosening them. On spaceboats such a precaution was usual.

"Give me two minutes," said Hoddan over his shoulder. "I have to get what they sent me for. After that everybody starts even."

He entered and closed the door behind him. Then he locked it. By the nature of things it is as needful to be able to lock a spaceboat from the inside as it is unnecessary to lock it from without.

He looked things over. Standard equipment everywhere. He checked everything, even to the fuel supply. There were knockings on the port. He continued to inspect. He turned on the vision screens, which provided the control-room and the rest of the boat with an unobstructed view in all directions. He was satisfied.

The knocks became bangings. Something approaching indignation could be deduced. The guards around the spaceboat felt that Hoddan was taking an unfair amount of time to pick the cream of the loot inside.

He got a glass of water. It was excellent. A second.

The bangings became violent hammerings.

Hoddan seated himself leisurely in the pilot's seat and turned small knobs. He waited. He touched a button. There was a mildly thunderous bang outside, and the lifeboat reacted as if to a slight shock. The vision screens showed a cloud of dust at the space-boat's stern, roused by a deliberate explosion in the rocket tubes. It also showed the retainers in full flight.

He waited until they were in safety and made the standard take-off preparations. A horrific roaring started up outside. He touched controls and a monstrous weight pushed him back in his seat. The rocket swung, lifted, and shot skyward with greater acceleration than before.

It went up at a lifeboat's full fall-like rate of climb, leaving a trail of blue-white flame behind it. All the surface of Darth seemed to contract swiftly below. The spaceport and the town rushed toward a spot beneath the spaceboat's tail. They shrank and shrank. He saw other places. Mountains. Castles. He saw Don Loris' stronghold. Higher, he saw the sea.

The sky turned purple. It went black with specks of star-shine in it. Hoddan swung to a westward course and continued to rise, watching the star images as they shifted on the screens. The image of the sun, of course, was automatically diminished so that it was not dazzling. The rockets continued to roar, though in a minor fashion because there was no longer air outside in which a bellow could develop.

Hoddan painstakingly made use of those rule-of-thumb methods of astrogation which his piratical fathers had developed and which a boy on Zan absorbed without being aware. He wanted an orbit around Darth. He didn't want to take time to try to compute it. So he watched the star-images ahead and astern. If the stars ahead rose above the planet's edge faster than those behind sank down below it, he would be climbing. If the stars behind sank down faster than those ahead rose up, he would be descending. If all the stars rose equally he'd be climbing straight up, and if they all dropped equally he'd be moving straight down. It was not a complex method, and it worked.

Presently he relaxed. He sped swiftly toward the sunrise line on Darth. This was the reverse of a normal orbit, but it was the direction followed by the ships up here. He hoped his orbit was lower than theirs. If it was, he'd overtake them from behind. If he were higher, they'd overtake him.

He turned on the spacephone. Its reception indicator was piously placed at *ground*. He shifted it to space, so that it would pick up calls going planetward, instead of listening vainly for replies from the non-operative landing-grid.

Instantly voices boomed in his ears. Many voices. An impossibly large number of voices. Many, many, many more than nine transmitters were in operation now!

"Idiot!" said a voice in quiet passion, "sheer off or you'll get in our drive-field!" A high-pitched voice said, "—and group two take second orbit position." Somebody bellowed, "But why don't they answer?" And another voice still, said formally, "Reporting group five, but four ships are staying behind with tanker, *Toya,* which is having stabilizer trouble."

Hoddan's eyes opened very wide. He turned down the sound while he tried to think. But there wasn't anything to think. He'd come aloft to scout three ships that had turned to nine, because he was in such a fix on Darth that anything strange might be changed into something useful. But this was more than nine ships—itself an impossibly large space-fleet. There was no reason why ships of space should ever travel together. There were innumerable reasons why they shouldn't. There was a limit to the number of ships that could be accommodated at any spaceport in the galaxy. There was no point, no profit, no purpose in a number of ships traveling together.

Darth's sunrise-line appeared far ahead. The lifeboat would soon cease to be a bright light in the sky, now. The sun's image vanished from the rear screens. The boat went hurtling onward through the blackness of the planet's shadow while voices squabbled, wrangled, and formally reported.

During the period of darkness, Hoddan racked his brains for the vaguest of ideas on why so many ships should appear about an obscure and unimportant world like Darth. Presently the sunset-line appeared ahead, and far away he saw moving lights which were the hulls of the volubly communicating vessels. He stared, blankly. There were tens. Scores. He was forced to guess at the stark impossibility of more than a hundred spacecraft in view. As the boat rushed onward he had to raise the guess. It couldn't be, but—

He turned on the outside telescope, and the image on its screen was more incredible than the voices and the existence of the fleet itself. The scope focused first on a bulging, monster. It was an antiquated freighter that had not been built for a hundred years. The second view was of a passenger-liner with the elaborate ornamentation that in past generations was considered suitable for space. There was a bulk-cargo ship, with no emergency rockets at all and the crew's quarters in long blisters built outside the gigantic tank which was the ship itself. There was a needle-like spaceyacht. More freighters, with streaks of rust on their sides where they had lain aground for tens of years.

The fleet was an anomaly, and each of its component parts was a separate freak. It was a gathering together of all the outmoded and obsolete hulks and monstrosities of space. One would have to scavenge half the galaxy to bring together so many crazy, over-age derelicts that should have been in junk yards.

Then Hoddan drew an explosive deep breath. It was suddenly clear what the fleet was and what its reason must be. Why it stopped here, he could not yet guess.

Hoddan watched absorbedly. There was some emergency. It could be in the line of what an electronic engineer could handle.

# CHAPTER VII

The spaceboat floated on upon a collision course with the arriving fleet. That would not mean, of course, actual contact with any of the strange vessels themselves. Crowded as the sunlit specks might seem from Darth's night-side shadow, they were sufficiently separated. It was more than likely that even with ten-mile intervals the ships would be considered much too crowded. But they came pouring out of emptiness to go into a swirling, plainly pre-intended orbit about the planet from which Hoddan had risen less than an hour before.

It was a gigantic traffic tangle, and Hoddan's boat drifted toward and into it. He'd counted a hundred ships long before. His count now passed two hundred and continued. Before he gave up, he'd numbered two hundred forty-seven of the oddities swarming to make a whirling band—a ring—around the planet Darth.

He was fairly sure that he knew what they were, now. But he could not possibly guess where they came from. And most mysterious of all was the question of why they'd come out of faster-than-light drive to make of themselves a celestial feature about a planet which had practically nothing to offer to anybody.

Presently the spaceboat was in the very thick of the fleet. His communicator spouted voices whose tones ranged from basso profundo to high tenor, and whose ideas of proper astrogation seemed to vary more widely still.

"You there!" boomed a voice with deafening volume. "You're in our clear-space! Sheer off!"

The volume of a signal in space varies as the square of the distance. This voice was thunderous. It came apparently from a nearby, potbellied ship of ancient vintage.

Hoddan's spaceboat floated on. The relative position of the two ships changed slowly. Another voice said indignantly:

"That's the same thing that missed us by less than a mile! You, there! Stop acting like a squig! Get on your own course!"

A third voice:

"What boat's that? I don't recognize it! I thought I knew all the freaks in this fleet, too!"

A fourth voice said sharply:

"That's not one of us! Look at the design! That's not us!"

Other voices broke in. There was babbling. Then a harsh voice roared:

"Quiet! I order it!" There was silence. The harsh voice said heavily, "Relay the image to me." There was a pause. The same voice said grimly: "It is not of our fleet. You, stranger! Identify yourself! Who are you and why did you slip secretly among us?"

Hoddan pushed the transmit button.

"My name is Bron Hoddan," he said. "I came up to find out why three ships, and then nine ships, went into orbit around Darth. It was somewhat alarming. Our landing-grid's disabled, anyhow, and it seemed wisest to look you over before we communicated and possibly told you something you might not believe." The harsh voice said as grimly as before:

"You come from the planet below us? Darth? Why is your ship so small? The smallest of ours is greater."

"This is a lifeboat," said Hoddan pleasantly. "It's supposed to be carried on larger ships in case of emergency."

"If you will come to our leading ship," said the voice, "we will answer all your questions. I will have a smoke flare set off to guide you."

Hoddan said to himself:

*No threats and no offers. I can guess why there are no threats. But they should offer something!*

He waited. There was a sudden, huge eruption of vapor in space some two hundred miles away. Perhaps an ounce of explosion had been introduced into a rocket tube and fired. The smoke particles, naturally ionized, added their self-repulsion to the expansiveness of the explosive's gases. A cauliflower-like shape of filmy whiteness appeared and grew larger and thinner.

Hoddan drove toward the spot. He swung the boat around and killed its relative velocity. The leading ship was a sort of gigantic, shapeless, utterly preposterous ark-like thing. Hoddan could neither imagine a purpose for which it could have been used, nor a time when men would have built anything like it. Its huge sides seemed to be made exclusively of great doorways now tightly closed.

One of those doorways gaped wide. It would have admitted a good-sized modern ship. A nervous voice essayed to give Hoddan directions for getting the spaceboat inside what was plainly an enormous hold now pumped empty of air. He grunted and made the attempt. It was tricky. He sweated when he cut off his power. But he felt fairly safe. Rocket flames would burn down such a door, if necessary. He could work havoc if hostilities began.

The great door swung shut. The outside-pressure needle swung sharply and stopped at thirty centimetres of mercury pressure. There was a clanging. A smaller door evidently opened somewhere. Lights came on. Then figures appeared through a door leading to some other part of this ship.

Hoddan nodded to himself. The costume was odd. It was awkward. It was even primitive, but not in the fashion of the soiled, gaudily-colored garments of Darth. These men wore unrelieved black, with gray shirts. There was no touch of color about them. Even the younger ones wore beards. And of all unnecessary things, they wore flat-brimmed hats—in a spaceship!

Hoddan opened the door and said politely:

"Good morning. I'm Bron Hoddan. You were talking to me."

The oldest and most fiercely bearded of the men said harshly:

"I am the leader here. We are the people of Colin." He frowned when Hoddan's expression remained unchanged. "The people of Colin!" he repeated more loudly. "The people whose forefathers settled that planet, and made it a world of peace and plenty, and then foolishly welcomed strangers to their midst!"

"Too bad," said Hoddan. He knew what these people were doing, he believed, but putting a name to where they'd come from told him nothing of what they wanted of Darth.

"We made it a fair world," said the bearded man fiercely. "But it was my great-grandfather who destroyed it. He believed that we should share it. It was he who persuaded the Synod to allow strangers to settle among us, believing that they would become like us."

Hoddan nodded expectantly. These people were in some sort of trouble or they wouldn't have come out of overdrive. But they'd talked about it until it had become an emotionalized obsession that couldn't be summarized. When they encountered a stranger, they had to picture their predicament passionately and at length.

This bearded man looked at Hoddan with burning eyes. When he went on, it was with gestures as if he were making a speech. But it was a special sort of speech. The first sentence told what kind.

"They clung to their sins!" said the bearded man bitterly. "They did not adopt our ways! Our example went for naught! They brought others of their kind to Colin. After a little they laughed at us. In a little more they outnumbered us! Then they ruled that the laws of our Synod should not govern them. And they lured our young people to imitate them-frivolous, sinful, riotous folk that they were!"

Hoddan nodded again. There were elderly people on Zan who talked like this. Not *his* grandfather! If you listened long enough they'd come to some point or other, but they had arranged their thoughts so solidly that any attempt to get quickly at their meaning would only produce confusion.

"Twenty years since," said the bearded man with an angry gesture, "we made a bargain. We held a third of all the land of the planet, but our young men were falling away from the ways of their fathers. We made a bargain with the newcomers. We would trade our lands, our cities, our farms, our highways, for ships to take us to a new world, and food for the journey and machines for the taming of the planet we would select. We sent some of our number to find a world to which we could move. Ten years back, they returned. They had found it. The planet Thetis."

Again Hoddan had no reaction. The name meant nothing.

"We began to prepare," said the old man, his eyes flashing. "Five years since, we were ready. But we had to wait three more before the bargainers were ready to complete the trade. They had to buy and collect the ships. They had to design and build the machinery we would need. They had to collect the food supplies. Two years ago we moved our animals into the ships, and loaded our food and our furnishings, and took our places. We set out. For two years we have journeyed toward Thetis."

Hoddan felt an instinctive respect for people who would undertake to move themselves, the third of the population of a planet, over a distance that meant years of voyaging. They might have tastes in costume that he did not share, and they might go in for elaborate oratory instead of matter-of-fact statements, but they had courage.

"Yes, sir," said Hoddan. "I take it this brings us up to the present."

"No," said the old man. "Six months ago we considered that we might well begin to train the operators of the machines we would use on Thetis. We uncrated machines. We found ourselves cheated!"

Hoddan found that he could make a fairly dispassionate guess of what advantage—say—Nedda's father would take of people who would not check on his good faith for two years and until they were two years' journey away.

"How badly were you cheated?" asked Hoddan.

"Of our lives!" said the angry old man. "Do you know machinery?"

"Some kinds," admitted Hoddan.

"Come," said the leader of the fleet.

With a sort of dignity that was theatrical only because he was aware of it, the leader of the people of Colin showed the way. The hold was packed tightly with cases of machinery. One huge crate had been opened and its contents fully disclosed. Others had been hacked at enough to show their contents.

The uncrated machine was a jungle plow. It was a powerful piece of equipment which would attack jungle on a thirty-foot front, knock down all vegetation up to trees of four-foot diameter, shred it, loosen and sift the soil to a three-foot depth, and leave behind it smoothed, broken, pulverized dirt mixed with ground-up vegetation ready to break down into humus. Such a machine would clear tens of acres in a day, turning jungle into farm land ready for crops.

"We ran this for five minutes," said the bearded man fiercely as Hoddan nodded. He lifted a motor hood.

The motors were burned out. Worthless insulation. Gears were splintered and smashed, Low-grade metal castings. Assembly-bolts had parted. Tractor treads were bent and cracked. It was not a machine except in shape. It was a mock-up in worthless materials which probably cost its maker the twentieth part of what an honest jungle plow would cost to build.

Hoddan felt the anger any man feels when he sees betrayal of that honor a competent machine represents.

"It's not all like this!" he said incredulously.

"Some is worse," said the old man, with dignity. "There are crates which are marked to contain turbines. Their contents are ancient, worn-out brick-making machines. There are crates marked to contain generators. They are filled with corroded irrigation pipes and broken castings. We have shiploads of crush-baled, rusted sheet-metal trimmings! We have been cheated of our lives!"

Hoddan found himself sick with honest fury. The population of one-third of a planet, packed into spaceships for two years and more, would be appropriate subjects for sympathy at the best of times. But it was only accident that had kept these people from landing on Thetis by rocket—since none of their ships would be expected ever to rise again—and from having their men go out and joyfully hack at alien jungle to make room for their machines to land—and then find out they'd brought scrap metal for some thousands of light-years to no purpose.

They'd have starved outright. In fact, they were in not much better case right now. Because there was nowhere else that they could go! There was no new colony which could absorb so many people, with only their bare hands for equipment to live by. There was no civilized, settled world which could admit so many paupers without starving its own population. There was nowhere for these people to go!

Hoddan's anger took on the feeling of guilt. He could do nothing, and something had to be done.

"Why—why did you come to Darth?" he asked. "What can you gain by orbiting here? You can't expect—"

The old man faced him.

"We are beggars," he said with bitter dignity. "We stopped here to ask for charity…for the old and worn-out machines the people of Darth can spare us. We will be grateful for even a single rusty plow. Because we have to go on. We can do nothing else. We will land on Thetis. And one plow can mean that a few of us will live who would otherwise die."

Hoddan ran his hands through his hair. This was not his trouble, but he could not ignore it.

"But again, why Darth?" he asked helplessly. "Why not stop at a world with riches to spare? Darth's a poor place."

"Because it is the poor who are generous," said the bearded man evenly.

Hoddan paced up and down. Presently he said jerkily:

"With all the good will in the world… Darth is poverty-stricken. It has no industries. It has no technology. It has not even roads! It is a planet of little villages and tiny towns. A ship from elsewhere stops here only once a month. Ground communications are almost non-existent. To spread the word of your need over Darth would require months. But to collect what might be given, without roads or even wheeled vehicles—it's impossible! And I have the only space-vessel on the planet, and it's not fit for a journey between suns."

The bearded man waited with a sort of implacable despair.

"But," continued Hoddan grimly, "I have an idea. I have contacts on Walden. The government of Walden does not regard charity with favor. The need for charity seems a—ah—a criticism of the Waldenian standard of living."

The bearded man said coldly:

"I can understand that. The hearts of the rich are hardened. The existence of the poor is a reproach to them."

But Hoddan began suddenly to see real possibilities. This was not a direct move toward the realization of his personal ambitions. But on the other hand, it wasn't a movement away from them. Hoddan suddenly remembered an oration he'd heard his grandfather give many, many times in the past.

*Straight thinkin'*, the old man had said obstinately, *is a delusion. You think things out clear and simple, and you can see yourself ruined and your family starving any day! Real things ain't simple! Any time you try to figure things out so they's simple and straightforward, you're goin' against nature and you're going to get 'em mixed up! So when something happens and you're in a straightforward, hopeless fix, why, you go along with nature! Make it as complicated as you can, and the people who want you in trouble will get hopeless confused and you can get out!*

Hoddan adverted to his grandfather's wisdom, not making it the reason for doing what he could, but accepting the fact that it might possibly apply. He saw one possibility right away. It looked fairly good. After a minute's examination it looked better. It was astonishing how plausible…

"Hmmmmmm," he said. "I have planned work of my own, as you may have guessed. I am here because of—ah—people on Walden. If I could make a quick trip to Walden my—hm—present position might let me help you. I cannot promise very much, but if I can borrow even the smallest of your ships for the journey my spaceboat can't make, why, I may be able to do something. Much more than can be done on Darth!"

The bearded man looked at his companions.

"He seems frank," he said, "and we can lose nothing. We have stopped our journey and are in orbit. We can wait. Our people should not go to Walden. Fleshpots—"

"I can find a crew," said Hoddan cheerfully. Inwardly he was tremendously relieved. "If you say the word, I'll go down to ground and come back with them. I'll want a very small ship!"

"It will be," said the old man. "We thank you."

"Get it inboard, here," suggested Hoddan, "so I can come inside as before, transfer my crew without spacesuits, and leave my boat in your care until I come back."

"It shall be done," said the old man firmly. He added gravely, "You must have had an excellent upbringing, young man, to be willing to live among the poverty-stricken people you describe, and to be willing to go so far to help strangers like ourselves."

"Eh?" Then Hoddan said enigmatically. "What lessons I shall apply to your affairs, I learned at the knee of my beloved grandfather."

Of course, his grandfather was head of the most notorious gang of pirates on the disreputable planet Zan, but Hoddan found himself increasingly respectful of the old gentlemen as he gained experience on various worlds.

He went briskly back to his spaceboat. On the way he made verbal arrangements for the enterprise he'd envisioned so swiftly. It was remarkable how two sets of troubles could provide suggestions for their joint alleviation. He actually saw possible achievement before him. Even in electronics!

By the time the cargo-hold was again pumped empty and the great door opened to the vastness of space, Hoddan had a very broad view of things. He'd said that same day to Fani that a practical man can always make what he wants to do look like a sacrifice for others' welfare. He began to suspect, now, that the welfare of others can often coincide with one's own.

He needed some rather extensive changes in the relationship of the cosmos to himself. Walden was prepared to pay bribes for him. Don Loris felt it necessary to have him confined somewhere. There were a number of Darthian gentlemen who would assuredly like to slaughter him if he weren't kept out of their reach in some cozy dungeon. But up to now there had been not even a practical way to leave Darth, to act upon Walden, or even to change his status in the eyes of Darthians.

He backed out of the big ship and consulted the charts of the lifeboat. They had been consulted before, of course, to locate the landing-grid which did not answer calls. He found its position. He began to compare the chart with what he saw from out here in orbit above Darth. He identified a small ocean, with Darth's highest mountain chain just beyond its eastern limit. He identified a river system, emptying into that sea. And here he began to get rid of his excess velocity, because the landing-grid was not very far distant.

To a scientific pilot, his maneuvering from that time on would have been a complex task. The advantage of computation over astrogation by ear, however, is largely a matter of saving fuel. A perfectly computed course for landing will get down to ground with the use of the least number of centigrams of fuel. But fuel-efficient maneuvers are rarely time-efficient ones.

Hoddan hadn't the time or the data for computation. He swung the spaceboat end for end, very judgematically used rocket power to slow himself to a suitable east-west velocity, and at the last and proper instant applied full power for deceleration and went down practically like a stone. One cannot really learn this. It has to be absorbed through the pores of one's skin. That was the way Hoddan had absorbed it, on Zan.

Within minutes, then, the stronghold of Don Loris was startled by a roaring mutter in the sky overhead. Helmeted sentries on the battlements stared upward. The mutter rose to a howl, and the howl to the volume of thunder, and the thunder to a very great noise which made loose pebbles dance and quiver.

Then there was a speck of white cloudiness in the late afternoon sky. It grew swiftly in size, and a winking blue-white light appeared in its center. That light grew brighter and the noise managed somehow to increase and presently the ruddy sunlight was diluted by light from the rockets.

Then, abruptly, the rockets cut off, and something dark plunged downward, and the rockets flamed again and a vast mass of steam arose from scorched ground. The spaceboat lay in a circle of wildly smoking, carbonized Darthian soil. The return of tranquility after so much tumult was startling.

Absolutely nothing happened. Hoddan unstrapped himself from the pilot's seat, examined his surroundings thoughtfully, and turned off the vision apparatus. He went back and examined the feeding arrangements of the boat. He'd had nothing to eat since breakfast in this same time zone. The food in store was extremely easy to prepare and not especially appetizing. He ate with great deliberation, continuing to make plans which linked the necessities of the emigrants from Colin to his own plans and predicaments. He also thought very respectfully about his grandfather's opinions on many subjects, including space-piracy. Hoddan found himself much more in agreement with his grandfather than he'd believed possible.

Outside the boat, birds which had dived to ground and cowered there during the boat's descent now flew about again, their terror forgotten. Horses which had galloped wildly in their pastures, or kicked in panic in the castle stalls, returned to their oats and hay.

And there were human reactions. Don Loris had been in an excessively fretful state of mind since the conclusion of his deal with the pair from Walden. Hoddan had estimated that Don Loris ought to get a half-million credits for delivering him to Derec and the Waldenian police. But actually Don Loris had been unable to get the cop to promise more than half so much. But he'd closed the deal and sent for Hoddan—and Hoddan was gone.

Now the landing of this spaceboat roused a lively uneasiness in Don Loris. It might be new bargainers for Hoddan. It might be anything. Hoddan had said he had a secret. This might be it. Don Loris vexedly tried to contrive some useful skullduggery without the information to base it on.

Fani looked at the spaceboat with bright eyes. Thal was back at the castle. He'd told her of Hoddan riding up to the spaceboat near another chieftain's castle, entering it, and then taking to the skies in an aura of flames, smoke and thunder. Fani hoped that he might have returned. But she worried while she waited for him to do something.

Hoddan did nothing. The spaceboat gave no sign of life.

The sun set, and the sky twinkled with darting lights which flew toward the west and vanished. Twilight followed, and more lights flashed across the heavens as if pursuing the sun. Fani had learned to associate three and then nine such lights with spacecraft, but she could not dream of a fleet of hundreds. She dismissed the lights from her mind, being much more concerned with Hoddan. He would be in as bad a fix as ever if he came out of the boat.

Twilight remained, a half-light in which all things looked much more charming than they really were. And Don Loris, reduced to peevish sputtering, summoned Thal. It should be remembered that Don Loris knew nothing of the disappearance of the spaceboat from his neighbor's land. He knew nothing of Thal's journey with Hoddan. But he did remember that Hoddan had seemed unworried at breakfast and explained his calm by saying that he had a secret. The feudal chieftain was worried that this spaceboat contained Hoddan's secret.

"Thal," said Don Loris peevishly, sitting beside the great fireplace in the enormous hall. "Thal, you know this Bron Hoddan better than anybody else."

Thal breathed heavily. He turned pale.

"Where is he?" demanded Don Loris.

"I don't know," said Thal. It was true. So far as he was concerned, Hoddan had vanished into the sky.

"What does he plan to do?" demanded Don Loris.

"I don't know," said Thal helplessly.

"Where does that—that thing outside the castle come from?"

"I don't know," said Thal.

Don Loris drummed on the arm of his intricately carved chair.

"I don't like people who don't know things!" he said fretfully. "There must be somebody in that *thing*. Why don't they show themselves? What are they here for? Why did they come down, especially here? Because of Bron Hoddan?"

"I don't know," said Thal humbly.

"Then go find out!" snapped Don Loris. "Take a reasonable guard with you. The thing must have a door. Knock on it and ask who's inside and why they came here. Tell them I sent you to ask."

Thal saluted. With his teeth chattering, he gathered a half-dozen of his fellows and went tramping out the castle gate. Some of the half-dozen had been involved in the rescue of the Lady Fani from Ghek. They were still in a happy mood because of the plunder they'd brought back. It was much more than a mere retainer could usually hope for in a year.

"What's this all about, Thal?" demanded one of them as Thal arranged them in two lines to make a proper military appearance, spears dressed upright and shields on their left arms.

"Frrrrd *harch!*" barked Thal, and they swung into motion. Thal said gloomily, "Don Loris said to find out who landed that thing out yonder. He keeps asking about Bron Hoddan, too."

He strode in step with the others. The seven men made an impressively soldierly group, tramping away from the castle wall.

"What happened to him?" asked a rear-file man. He marched on, eyes front, chest out, spear swinging splendidly in time with his marching. "That lad has a nose for loot! Don't take it himself, though. If he set up in business as a chieftain, now—"

"Hup, two, three, four," muttered Thal. "Hup, two, three—"

"Don Loris's a hard chieftain," growled the right-hand man in the second file. "Plenty of grub and beer, but no fighting and no loot. I didn't get to go with you the other day, but what you brought back…"

"Wasn't half of what was there," mourned a front-file man. "Wasn't half! Those pistols he issued got shot out and we had to get outta there fast! Hm…here's this thing, Thal. What do we do with it?"

"Hrrrmp, *halt!*" barked Thal. He stared at the motionless, seemingly lifeless, shapeless spaceboat. He'd seen one like it earlier today. That one spouted fire and went up out of sight. He was wary of this one. He grumbled. "Those pipes in the back of it, steer clear of 'em. They spit fire. No door on this side. Don Loris said knock on the door. We go around the front. Frrrrd *harch!* two, three, four, *hup,* two, three, four. Left turn here and mind those rocks. Don Loris'd give us hell if somebody fell down. Left turn again, *Hup,* two, three, four."

The seven men tramped splendidly around the front of the lifeboat. On the far side, its bulk hid even Don Loris' castle from view. The six spearmen, with Thal, came to a second halt.

"Here goes," rumbled Thal. "I tell you, boys, if she starts to spit fire, you get the hell away!"

He marched up to spaceboat's port. He knocked on it. There was no response. He knocked again.

Hoddan opened the door. He nodded cheerfully to Thal.

"Afternoon, Thal! Glad to see you. I've been hoping you'd come over this way. Who's with you?" He peered through the semi-darkness. "Some of the boys, eh? Come in!" He beckoned and said casually, "Lean your spears against the hull, there."

Thal hesitated and was lost. The others obeyed. There were clatterings as the spears came to rest against the metal hull. Six of Don Loris' retainers followed Thal admiringly into the spaceboat's interior, to gaze at it and at Bron Hoddan who so recently had given them the chance to loot a nearby castle.

"Sit down!" said Hoddan cordially. "If you want to feel what a spaceboat's really like, clasp the seat-belts around you. You'll feel exactly like you're about to make a journey out of atmosphere. That's it, lean back. You notice there are no viewports in the hull? That's because we use these vision screens to see around with."

He flicked on the screens. Thal and his companions were charmed to see the landscape outside portrayed on screens. Hoddan shifted the sensitivity point toward infrared, and details came out that would have been invisible to the naked eye.

"With the port closed," said Hoddan, "like this," the port clanged shut and grumbled for half a second as the locking-dogs went home, "we're all set for take-off. I need only get into the pilot's seat..." he did so, "and throw on the fuel pump." A tiny humming sounded. "And we move when I advance this throttle!"

He pressed the firing-stud. There was a soul-shaking roar. There was a terrific pressure. The seven men from Don Loris' stronghold were pressed back in their seats with an overwhelming, irresistible pressure which held them absolutely helpless. Their mouths dropped open. Appalled protests tried to come out, but were pushed back by the seemingly ever-increasing acceleration.

The screens, showing the outside, displayed a great and confused tumult of smoke and fumes and dust to rearward. They showed only stars ahead. Those stars grew brighter and brighter, as the roar of the rockets diminished to a deafening sound. Suddenly the disk of the local sun appeared, rising above the horizon to the west. The spaceboat, naturally, overtook it as it rose into an orbit headed east to west instead of the other way about Presently Hoddan turned off the fuel pump. He turned to look thoughtfully at the seven men. They were very pale. They all sat very still, because they could see in the vision-screens that a strange, mottled, again-sunlit surface flowed past them with an appalling velocity They were very much afraid that they knew what it was. They did. It was the surface of the planet Darth.

"I'm glad you boys came along," said Hoddan. "We'll catch up with the fleet in a moment or two. The pirate fleet, you know! I'm very pleased with you. Not many groundlings would volunteer for space-piracy, not even with the loot there is in it."

Thal choked slightly, but no one else made a sound. No one even protested. Protests would have been no use. There were looks of anguish, but nothing else. Hoddan was the only one in the spaceboat who had the least idea of how to get it down again. His passengers had to go along for the ride, no matter where it led.

Numbly, they waited for what would befall.

# CHAPTER VIII

Hoddan did not worry about his captive-followers. Soon he saw the weird spacefleet.

The spaceboat drew up alongside the gigantic hulk of the leader's ship. The seven Darthians were still numbed by their kidnapping and the situation in which they found themselves. They looked with dull eyes at the mountainous object they approached. It had actually been designed as a fighter-carrier of space, intended to carry smaller craft. It must have been sold for scrap a couple of hundred years since, and patched up for this emigration.

Hoddan waited for the huge door to open. It did. He headed into the opening, noticing as he did so that an object two or three times the size of the spaceboat was already there. It cut down the room for maneuvering, but a thing once done is easier thereafter. Hoddan got the boat inside, and there was a very small scraping and the great door closed before the boat could drift out again.

Hoddan turned to his victim-followers once the spaceboat was still.

"This," he said in a manner which could only be described as one of smiling ferocity, "this is a pirate ship, belonging to the pirate fleet we passed through on the way here. It's manned by characters so murderous that their leaders don't dare land anywhere away from their home star-cluster, or all the galaxy would combine against them, to exterminate them or be exterminated. You've joined that fleet. You're going to get out of this boat and march over to that ship yonder. Then you're going to be space-pirates under me."

They quivered, but did not protest.

"I'll try you for one voyage," he told them. "There will be plunder. There will be pirate revels. If you serve faithfully and fight well, I'll return you to Don Loris' stronghold with your loot after the one voyage. If you don't—" He grinned mirthlessly at them, "if you don't, out the airlock with you, to float forever between the stars. Understand?"

The last was pure savagery. They cringed. The outside-pressure meter went up to normal. Hoddan turned off the vision screens, so ending any views of the interior of the hold. He opened the port and went out. Sitting in something like continued paralysis in their seats, the seven spearmen of Darth heard his voice in conversation outside the boat. They could catch no words, but Hoddan's tone was strictly businesslike. He came back.

"All right," he said shortly. "Thal, march 'em over."

Thal gulped. He loosened his seat-belt. The enlistment of the seven in the pirate fleet was tacitly acknowledged. They were unarmed save for the conventional large knives at their belts.

"Frrrd, *harch!*" rasped Thal with a lump in his throat. "Two, three, four, *Hup,* two, three, four. *Hup…*"

Seven men marched dismally out of the spaceboat and down to the floor of the huge hold. Eyes front, chests out, throats dry, they marched to the larger but still small vessel that shared this hold compartment. They marched into that ship. Thal barked, "Hmmmmm *halt!*" and they stopped. They waited.

Hoddan came in very matter-of-factly only moments later. He closed the entrance port, so sealing the ship. He nodded approvingly.

"You can break ranks now," he said. "There's food and such stuff around. The ship's yours. But don't turn knobs or push buttons."

He went forward, and a door closed behind him.

He looked at the control board, and could have done with a little information himself. When the ship was built, generations ago, there'd been controls installed which would be quite useless now. When the present working instruments were installed, it had been done so hastily that the wires and relays behind them were not concealed, and it was these that gave him the clues to understand them.

The space-ark's door opened. Hoddan backed his ship out. Its rockets had surprising power. He reflected that the Lawlor drive wouldn't have been designed for this present ship, either. There'd probably been a quantity order for so many Lawlor drives, and they'd been installed on whatever needed a modern drive-system, which was every ship in the fleet. But since this was one of the smallest craft in the lot, with its low mass it should be fast.

"We'll see," he said to nobody in particular.

Out in emptiness, but naturally sharing the orbit of the ship from which it had just come, Hoddan tried it out tentatively. He got the feel of it. Then as a matter of simple, rule-of-thumb astrogation, he got from a low orbit to a five-diameter height where the Lawlor drive would hold by mere touches of rocket power. It was simply a matter of stretching the orbit to extreme eccentricity as all the ships went round the planet. After the fourth go round he was fully five diameters out at aphelion. He touched the drive button and everybody had that very peculiar disturbance of all their senses which accompanies going into overdrive. The small craft sped through emptiness at a high multiple of the speed of light.

Hoddan's knowledge of astrogation was strictly practical. He went over his ship. From a look at it outside he'd guessed that it once had been a yacht. Various touches inside verified that idea. There were two staterooms. All the space was for living and supplies. None was for cargo. He nodded. There was a faint mustiness about it. But there'd been a time when it was some rich man's pride.

He went back to the control-room to make an estimate. From the pilot's seat one could see a speck of brightness directly ahead. Infinitesimal dots of brightness appeared swiftly brighter and then darted outward. As they darted they disappeared because their motion became too swift to follow. There were, of course, methods of measuring this phenomenon so that one could get an accurate measure of one's speed in overdrive. Hoddan had no instrument for the purpose. But he had the feel of things. This was a very fast ship indeed, at full Lawlor thrust.

Presently he went out to the central cabin. His followers had found provisions. There were novelties—hydroponic fruit, for instance—and they'd gloomily stuffed themselves. They were almost resigned, now. Memory of the loot he'd led them to at

Ghek's castle inclined them to be hopeful. But they looked uneasy when he stopped where they were gathered.

"Well?" he said sharply.

Thal swallowed.

"We have been companions, Bron Hoddan," he said unhappily. "We fought together in great battles, two against fifty, and we plundered the slain."

"True enough," agreed Hoddan. If Thal wanted to edit his memories of the fighting at the spaceport, that was all right with him. "Now we're headed for something much better."

"But what?" asked Thal miserably. "Here we are high above our native world—"

"Oh, no!" said Hoddan. "You couldn't even pick out its sun, from where we are now!"

Thal gulped.

"I do not understand what you want with us," he protested. "We are not experienced in space! We are simple men..."

"You're pirates now," Hoddan told him with a sort of genial bloodthirstiness. "You'll do what I tell you until we fight. Then you'll fight well or die. That's all you need to know!"

He left them. When men are to be led it is rarely wise to discuss policy or tactics with them. Most men work best when they know only what is expected of them. Then they can't get confused and they do not get ideas of how to do things better.

Hoddan inspected the yacht more carefully. There were still traces of decorative features which had nothing to do with spaceworthiness. But the mere antiquity of the ship made Hoddan hunt more carefully. He found a small compartment packed solidly with supplies. A supply cabinet did not belong where it was. He hauled out stuff to make sure. It was—it had been—a machine shop in miniature. In the early days, before space-phones were long-range devices, a yacht or a ship that went beyond orbital distance was strictly on its own. If there were a breakdown it was strictly of private concern. It had to be repaired by its own, or else. So all early spacecraft carried amazingly complete equipment for repairs. Only liners had been equipped that way in recent generations, and it is almost unheard of for their tool shops to be used.

But there was the remnant of a shop on the yacht that Hoddan was using for his errand to Walden. He'd told the emigrant leaders that he went to ask for charity. He'd just assured his followers that their journey was for piracy. Now…

He began to empty the cubbyhole of all the items that had been packed into it for storage. It had been very ingenious, this miniature repair shop. The lathe was built in with strength-members of the walls as part of its structure. The drill press was recessed. The welding apparatus had its coils and condensers under the floor. The briefest of examinations showed the condensers to be in bad shape, and the coils might be hopeless. But there was good material used in the old days. Hoddan began to have quite unreasonable hopes.

He went back to the control-room to meditate.

He'd had a reasonably sound plan of action for the pirating of a spaceliner, even though he had no weapons mounted on the ship nor anything more deadly than stun-pistols for his reluctant crew. But he considered it likely that he could make the same sort of landing with this yacht that he'd already done with the spaceboat. Which should be enough.

If he waited off Walden until a liner went down to the planet's great spaceport, he could try it. He would go into a close orbit around Walden which would bring him, very low, over the landing-grid within an hour or so of the liner's landing. He'd turn the yacht end for end and apply full rocket power for deceleration. The yacht would drop like a stone into the landing-grid. Everything would happen too quickly for the grid crew to think of clapping a forcefield on it, or for them to manage it if they tried. He'd be aground before they realized it.

The rest was simply fast action. Hoddan and seven Darthians, stun-pistols humming, would tumble out of the yacht and dash for the control-room of the grid. Hoddan would smash the controls. Then they'd rush the landed liner, seize it, shoot down anybody who tried to oppose them, and seal up the ship.

And then they'd take off on the liner's rockets, which were carried for emergency landing only, but could be used for a single take-off. After one such use they'd be exhausted. And with the grid's controls smashed, nobody could even try to stop them.

It wasn't a bad idea. He had a good deal of confidence in it. It was the reason for his Darthian crew. Nobody'd expect such a thing to be tried, so it almost certainly could be done. But it did have the drawback that the yacht would have to be left behind, a dead loss, when the liner was seized.

Hoddan thought it over soberly. Long before he reached Walden, of course, he could have his own crew so terrified that they'd fight like fiends for fear of what he might do to them if they didn't. But if he could keep the spaceyacht also...

He nodded gravely. He liked the new possibility. If it didn't work, there was the first plan in reserve. In any case he'd get a modern spaceliner and suitable cargo to present to emigrants of Colin.

There were certain electronic circuits which were akin. The Lawlor drive unit formed a forcefield, a stress in space, into which a nearby ship necessarily moved. The faster-than-light angle came from the fact that it worked like a donkey trotting after a carrot held in front of him by a stick. The ship moving into the stressed area moved the stress. The force-fields of a landing-grid were similar. A tuning principle was involved, but basically a landing-grid clamped an area of stress around a spaceship, and the ship couldn't move out of it. When the landing-grid moved the stressed area up or down—why—that was it.

All this was known to everybody. But a third trick had been evolved on Zan. It was based on the fact that ball lighting could be generated by a circuit fundamentally akin to the other two. Ball lightning was an area of space so stressed that its energy content could leak out only very slowly, unless it made contact with a conductor, when all bets were off. It blew. And the Zan pirates used ball lightning to force the surrender of their victims.

Hoddan began to draw diagrams. The Lawlor drive unit had been installed long after the yacht was built. It would be modern, with no nonsense about it. With such-and-such of its electronic components cut out, and such-and-such other ones cut in, it would become a perfectly practical ball-lightning generator, capable of placing bolts wherever one wanted them. This was standard Zan practice. Hoddan's grandfather had used it for years. It had the advantage that it could be used inside a gravity field, where a

Lawlor drive could not. It had the other advantage that commercial spacecraft could not mount such gadgets for defense, because the insurance companies objected to meddling with Lawlor drive installations.

Hoddan set to work with the remnants of a tool shop on the ancient yacht and some antique coils and condensers and such. He became filled with zest. He almost forgot that he was the skipper of an elderly craft which should have been junked before he was born.

But even he grew hungry, and he realized that nobody offered him food. He went indignantly into the yacht's central saloon and found his seven crew members snoring stertorously, sprawled in stray places here and there.

He woke them with great sternness. He set them furiously to work on housekeeping—including making meals.

He went back to work. Suddenly he stopped and meditated afresh, and ceased his actual labor to draw a diagram which he regarded with great affection. He returned to his adaptation of the Lawlor drive to the production of ball lightning.

Once finished, he examined the stars. The nearby suns were totally strange in their arrangement. But the Coalsack area was a spacemark good for half a sector of the galaxy. There was a condensation in the Nearer Rim for a second bearing. And a certain calcium cloud with a star-cluster behind it which was as good as a highway sign for locating oneself.

He lined up the yacht again and went into overdrive once more. Two days later he came out, again surveyed the cosmos, again went into overdrive, again came out, once more made a hop in faster-than-light travel, and finally he was in the solar system of which Walden was the ornament and pride.

He used the telescope and contemplated Walden on its screen. The spaceyacht moved briskly toward it. His seven Darthian crewmen, aware of coming action, dolefully sharpened their two-foot knives. They did not know what else to do, but they were far from happy.

Hoddan shared their depression. Such gloomy anticipations before stirring events are proof that a man is not a fool. Hoddan's grandfather had been known to observe that when a man can imagine all kinds of troubles and risks and disasters ahead of him, he is usually right. Hoddan shared that view. But it would not do to back out now.

He examined Walden painstakingly while the yacht sped towards it. He saw an ocean come out of the twilight zone of dawn. By the charts, the capitol city and the spaceport should be on that ocean's western shore. After a suitable and very long interval, the site of the capitol city came around the edge of the planet.

From a bare hundred thousand miles, Hoddan stepped up magnification to its limit and looked again. Then Walden more than filled the telescope's field. He could see only a very small fraction of the planet's surface. He had to hunt before he found the capitol city again. Then it was very clear. He saw the curving lines of its highways and the criss-cross pattern of its streets. Buildings as such, however, did not show. But he made out the spaceport and the shadow of the landing-grid, and in the very center of that grid there was something silvery which cast a shadow of its own. A ship. A liner.

Then the silvery thing moved visibly across other objects, and its shadow ceased to be. It was thrust surely and ever more swiftly skyward by the grid. The liner was rising to outer space.

There was a tap on the control-room door. Thal.

"Anything happening?" he asked uneasily.

"I just sighted the ship were going to take," said Hoddan.

Thal looked unhappy. He withdrew. Hoddan plotted out the extremely roundabout course he must take to end up with the liner and the yacht traveling in the same direction and the same speed, so capture would be possible. It could not be attempted in clear space. Five diameters out, the liner could whisk into overdrive and be gone forever. On the other hand, within five diameters the yacht couldn't use its drive, either. And yet again, the liner and the yacht had to be moving away from the planet at the time of capture, with enough velocity to attain clear space on their momentum, or there'd be no point in the attack. If the yacht did not float on out past the five-diameter limit, it could be gathered in by the landing-grid and brought to ground for such measures which might seem appropriate.

Hoddan worked out the angles and the speeds. He had to dive past Walden, swing around its farther side, and come back like a boomerang so his and the liner's speed and line of motion would match up into a collision course. Then rockets...

He put the yacht on the line required. He threw on full power. Actually, he headed partly away from his intended victim. The little yacht plunged forward. Nothing seemed to happen. Time passed. Hoddan had nothing to do but worry. He worried.

Thal tapped on the door again.

"About time to get ready to fight?" he asked dolefully.

"Not yet," said Hoddan. "I'm running away from our victim, now."

Another half-hour. The course changed. The yacht was around behind Walden. The whole planet lay between it and its intended prey. The course of the small ship curved, now. It would pass almost close enough to clip the topmost tips of Walden's atmosphere. There was nothing for Hoddan to do but think morbid thoughts. He thought them.

The Lawlor drive began to burble. He cut it off. He sat gloomily in the control-room, occasionally glancing at the nearing expanse of rushing mottled surface presented by the now-nearby planet. Its attraction bent the path of the yacht. It was now a parabolic curve.

Presently the surface diminished a little. The yacht was increasing its distance from it. Hoddan used the telescope. He searched the space ahead with full-width field. He found the liner. It rose steadily. The grid still thrust it upward with an even, continuous acceleration. It had to be not less than forty thousand miles out before it could take to overdrive. But at that distance it would have an outward velocity which would take it on out indefinitely. At ten thousand miles, certainly, the grid-fields would let go.

They did. Hoddan could tell because the liner wobbled slightly. It was free. It was no longer held solidly. From now on it floated up on momentum.

Hoddan nibbled at his fingernails. There was nothing to be done for forty minutes more. Presently there was nothing to be done for thirty. For twenty. Ten. Five. Three. Two—

The liner was barely twenty miles away when Hoddan fired his rockets. They made a colossal cloud of vapor in emptiness. The yacht stirred faintly, shifted deftly, lost just a suitable amount of velocity—which now was nearly straight up from the planet—and moved with precision and directness toward the liner. Hoddan stirred his controls and swung the whole small ship. He flipped a switch that cut out certain elements of the Lawlor unit and cut in those others which made the modified drive unit into a ball-lightning projector.

A flaming speck of pure incandescence sped from the yacht through emptiness. It would miss... No! Hoddan swerved it. It struck the liner's hull. It would momentarily paralyze every bit of electric equipment in the ship. It would definitely not go unnoticed.

"Calling liner," said Hoddan painfully into a microphone. "Calling liner! We are pirates, attacking your ship. You have ten seconds to get into your lifeboats or we will hull you!"

He settled back, again nibbling at his fingernails. He was acutely disturbed. At the end of ten seconds the distance between the two ships was perceptibly less.

He flung a second ball-lightning bolt across the diminished space. He sent it whirling round and round the liner in a tight spiral. He ended by having it touch the liner's bow. Liquid light ran over the entire hull.

"Your ten seconds are up," he said worriedly. "If you don't get out—" But then he relaxed. A boat-blister on the liner opened. The boat did not release itself. It could not possibly take on its complement of passengers and crew in so short a time. The opening of the blister was a sign of surrender.

The two first ball-lightning bolts were miniatures. Hoddan now projected a full-sized ball. It glittered viciously in emptiness. It sped toward the liner and hung off its side, menacingly. The yacht from Darth moved steadily closer. Five miles. Two.

"All out," said Hoddan regretfully. "We can't wait any longer!"

A boat darted away from the liner. A second. A third and fourth and fifth. The last boat lingered desperately. The yacht was less than a mile away when it broke free and plunged frantically toward the planet it had left a little while before. The other boats were already streaking downward, trails of rocket fumes expanding behind them. The crew of the landing-grid would pick them up for safe and gentle landing.

Hoddan sighed in relief. He played delicately upon the yacht's rocket controls. He carefully maneuvered the very last of the novelties he had build into the originally simple Lawlor drive unit. The two ships came together with a distinct clanking sound. It seemed horribly loud.

Thal jerked open the door, ashen white.

"W-we hit something! Wh-when do we fight?"

"I forgot. The fighting's over," Hoddan said ruefully. "But bring your stun-pistols. Nobody'd stay behind, but somebody might have gotten left."

He rose, to take over the captured ship.

# CHAPTER IX

Normally, at overdrive cruising speed, it would be a week's journey from Walden to the planet Krim. Hoddan made it in five days. There was reason. He wanted to beat the news of his piracy to Krim. He could endure suspicion, and he wouldn't mind doubt, but he did not want certainty of his nefarious behavior to interfere with the purposes of his call.

The spaceyacht, sealed tightly, floated in an orbit far out in emptiness. The big ship went down alone by landing-grid. It glittered brightly as it descended. When it touched ground and the grid's forcefields cut off, it looked very modern and very crisp and strictly businesslike. Actually, the capture of this particular liner was a bit of luck, for Hoddan. It was not one of the giant inter-cluster ships which make runs of thousands of light-years and deign to stop only at very major planets. It was a medium ship of five thousand tons, designed for service in the Horsehead Nebula region. It was brand-new and on the way from its builders to its owners when Hoddan interfered. Naturally, though, it carried cargo on its maiden voyage.

Hoddan spoke curtly to the control-room of the grid.

"I'm non-sked," he explained. "New ship. I got a freak charter-party over on Walden for from here for Darth and I have to get rid of my cargo. How about shifting me to a delay space until I can talk to some brokers?"

The forcefields came on again and the liner moved very delicately to a position at the side of the grid's central space. There it would be out of the way.

Hoddan dressed himself carefully in garments found in the liners skipper's cabin. He found Thal wearing an apron and an embittered expression. He ceased to wield a mop as Hoddan halted before him.

"I'm going ashore," said Hoddan crisply. "You're in charge until I get back."

"In charge of what?" demanded Thal bitterly. "Of a bunch of male housemaids! I run a mop! And me a Darthian gentleman! I thought I was being a pirate! What do I do? I scrub floors! I wash paint! I stencil cases in cargo-holds! I paint over names and put others in their places! Me, a Darthian gentleman!"

"No," said Hoddan. "A pirate. If you don't get back, you and the others can't work this ship, and presently the police of Krim will ask why. They'll re-check my careful forgeries, and you'll all be hung for piracy. So don't let anybody in. Don't talk to anybody. If you do, pfft!"

He drew his finger across his throat, and nodded, and went cheerfully out the crew's landing-door in the very base of the ship. He went across the tarmac and out between two of the gigantic steel arches of the grid. He hired a car.

"Where?" asked the driver.

"Hm," said Hoddan. "There's a firm of lawyers…I can't remember the names…

"There's millions of 'em," said the driver.

"This is a special one," explained Hoddan. "It's so dignified they won't talk to you unless you're a great-grandson of a client. They're so ethical they won't touch a case of under a million credits. They've got about nineteen names in the firm-title and—"

"Oh!" said the driver. "That'll be—Hell! I can't remember the name, either. But I'll take you there."

He drove out into traffic. Hoddan relaxed. Then he tensed again. He had not been in a city since he stopped briefly in this one on the way to Darth. The traffic was abominable. And he, who'd been in various pitched battles on Darth and had only lately captured a ship in space—Hoddan grew apprehensive as his cab charged into the thick of hooting, rushing, squealing vehicles. When the car came to a stop he was relieved.

"It's yonder," said the driver. "You'll find the name on the directory."

Hoddan paid and went inside the gigantic building. He looked at the directory and shrugged. He went to the downstairs guard. He explained that he was looking for a firm of lawyers whose name was not on the directory list. They were extremely conservative and of the highest possible reputation. They didn't seek clients.

"Forty-two and forty-three," said the guard, frowning. "I ain't supposed to give it out, but—floors forty-two and-three."

Hoddan went up. He was unknown. A receptionist looked at him with surprised aversion.

"I have a case of space-piracy," said Hoddan politely. "A member of the firm, please."

Ten minutes later he eased himself into a fluffy chair. A gray-haired man of infinite dignity said:

"Well?"

"I am," said Hoddan modestly, "a pirate. I have a ship in the spaceport with very convincing papers and a cargo of Rigellian furs, jewelry from the Cetis planets, and a rather large quantity of bulk *melacynth*. I want to dispose of the cargo and invest a considerable part of the proceeds in conservative stocks on Krim."

The lawyer frowned. He looked shocked. Then he said carefully:

"You made two statements. One was that you are a pirate. Taken by itself, that is not my concern. The other is that you wish to dispose of certain cargo and invest in reputable businesses on Krim. I assume that there is no connection between the two facts."

He paused. Hoddan said nothing. The lawyer went on, with dignity:

"Of course our firm is not in the brokerage business. However, we can represent you in your dealing with local brokers. And obviously we can advise you."

"I also wish to buy," said Hoddan, "a complete shipload of agricultural machinery, a microfilm technical library, machine tools, vision-tape technical instructors and libraries of tape for them, generators, and such things."

"Hm," said the lawyer, "I will send one of our clerks to examine your cargo so he can deal properly with the brokers. You will tell him more in detail what you wish to buy."

Hoddan stood up.

"I'll take him to the ship now."

He was mildly surprised at the smoothness with which matters proceeded. He took a young clerk to the ship. He showed him the ship's papers as edited by himself. He took him through the cargo holds. He discussed in some detail what he wished to buy.

When the clerk left, Thal came to complain again.

"Look here!" he said bitterly, "we've scrubbed this dam' ship from one end to the other! There's not a speck or a fingermark on it. And we're still scrubbing! We captured this ship! Is this pirate revels?"

Hoddan said:

"There's money coming. I'll let you boys ashore with some cash in your pockets presently."

Brokers came, escorted by the lawyer's clerk. They squabbled furiously with him. But the dignity of the firm he represented was extreme. There was no suspicion—no overt suspicion anyhow—and the furs went. The clerk painstakingly informed Hoddan that he could draw so much. More brokers came. The jewelry went. The lawyer's clerk jotted down figures and told Hoddan the net. The bulk *melacynth* was taken over by a group of brokers, none of whom could handle it alone.

Hoddan drew cash and sent his Darthians ashore with a thousand credits apiece. With bright and shining faces, they headed for the nearest bars.

"As soon as my ship's loaded," Hoddan told the clerk, "I'll want to get them out of jail."

The clerk nodded. He brought salesmen of agricultural machinery. Representatives of microfilm libraries. Manufacturers of generators, vision-tape instructors and allied lines. Hoddan bought, painstakingly. Delivery was promised for the next day.

"Now," said the clerk, "about the investments you wish to make with the balance?"

"I'll want a reasonable sum in cash," said Hoddan reflectively. "But—well...I've been told that insurance is a fine, conservative business. As I understand it, most insurance organizations are divided into divisions which are separately incorporated. There will be a life insurance division, a casualty division, and so on. Is that right? And one may invest in any of them separately?"

The clerk said impassively:

"I was given to understand, sir, that you are interested in risk insurance. Perhaps especially risk insurance covering piracy. I was given quotations on the risk insurance divisions of all Krim companies. Of course those are not very active stocks, but if there were a rumor of a pirate ship acting in this part of the galaxy, one might anticipate…

"I do," said Hoddan. "Let's see…my cargo brought so much…hm…my purchases will come to so much. My legal fees, of course… I mentioned a sum in cash. Yes. This will be the balance, more or less, which you will put in the stocks you've named. But since I anticipate activity in them, I'll want to leave some special instructions."

He gave a detailed, thoughtful account of what he anticipated might be found in news reports of later dates. The clerk noted it all down, impassively. Hoddan added instructions.

"Yes, sir," said the clerk without intonation when he was through. "If you will come to the office in the morning, sir, the papers will be drawn up and matters can be concluded. Your new cargo can hardly be delivered before then, and if I may say so, sir, your crew won't be ready. I'd estimate two hours of festivity for each man, and fourteen hours for recovery."

"Thank you," said Hoddan. "I'll see you in the morning."

He sealed up the ship when the lawyer's clerk departed. Then he felt lonely. He was the only living thing in the ship. His footsteps echoed hollowly. There was nobody to speak to. Not even anybody to threaten. He'd done a lot of threatening lately.

He went forlornly to the cabin once occupied by the liner's former skipper. His loneliness increased; he began to have self-doubts. Today's actions were the ones which bothered his conscience. He felt that they were not quite adequate. The balance left in the lawyer's hands would not be nearly enough to cover a certain deficit which in justice he felt himself bound to make up. It had been his thought to make this enterprise self-liquidating—everybody concerned making a profit, including the owners of the ship and cargo he had pirated. But he wasn't sure.

He reflected that his grandfather would not have been disturbed about such a matter. That elderly pirate would have felt wholly at ease. It was his conviction that piracy was an essential part of the working of the galaxy's economic system. Hoddan, indeed, could remember him saying:

"I tell y', piracy's what keeps the galaxy's business thriving. Everybody knows business suffers when retail trade slacks down. It backs up the movement of inventories. They get too big. That backs up orders to the factories. They lay off men. And when men are laid off they don't have money to spend, so retail trade slacks off some more, and that backs up inventories some more, and that backs up orders to factories and makes unemployment and hurts retail trade again. It's a feedback. See?" It was Hoddan's grandfather's custom, at this point, to stare shrewdly at each of his listeners in turn. "But suppose somebody pirates a ship? The owners don't lose. It's insured. They order another ship built right away. Men get hired to build it and they're paid money to spend in retail trade and that moves inventories and industry picks up. More'n that, more people insure against piracy. Insurance companies hire more clerks and bookkeepers. They get more money for retail trade and to move inventories and keep factories going and get more people hired. Y'see…it's piracy that keeps business in this galaxy goin'!"

Hoddan had doubts about this, but it could not be entirely wrong. He'd put a good part of the proceeds of his piracy in risk-insurance stocks, and he counted on them to make all his actions as benevolent to everybody concerned as his intentions had been, and were. But it might not be true enough. It might be less than—well—sufficiently true in a particular instance. And therefore—Then he saw how things could be worked out so that there could be no doubt. He began to work out the details. He drifted off to sleep in the act of composing a letter in his head to his grandfather on the pirate planet Zan.

When morning came on Krim, catawheel trucks came bringing gigantic agricultural machines. There came generators, turbines and tanks of plastic; another bevy of trucks brought vision-tape instructors and great boxes full of tape for them. There were machine tools and cutting-tips—these last in vast quantity—and very many items that the emigrants of Colin probably would not expect, and might not even recognize. The cargo holds of the liner filled.

He went to the office of his attorneys. He read and signed papers, in an atmosphere of great dignity and ethical purpose. The lawyer's clerk attended him to the police office, where seven dreary Darthians with over-sized hangovers tried dismally to cheer themselves by memories of how they got that way. He got them out and to the ship. The lawyer's clerk produced a rather weighty if small box with an air of extreme solemnity.

"The currency you wanted, sir."

"Thank you," said Hoddan. "That's the last of our business?"

"Yes, sir," said the clerk. He hesitated, and for the first time showed a trace of human curiosity. "Could I ask a question, sir, about piracy?"

"Why not?" asked Hoddan. "Go ahead."

"When you—ah—captured this ship, sir," said the clerk hopefully, "did you—ah—shoot the men and keep the women?"

Hoddan sighed.

"Much," he said regretfully, "much as I hate to spoil an enlivening theory—no. These are modern days. Efficiency has invaded even the pirate business. I used my crew for floor scrubbing and cooking."

He closed the port gently and went up to the control-room to call the landing-grid operators. In minutes the captured liner, loaded down again, lifted toward the stars.

And all the journey back to Darth was as anticlimactic as that. There was no trouble finding the spaceyacht in its remote orbit. Hoddan sent out an unlocking signal, and a keyed transmitter began to send a signal on which to home. When the liner nudged alongside it, Hoddan's last contrivance operated and the yacht clung fast to the larger ship's hull. There were four days in overdrive. There were three or four pauses for position-finding. The stopover on Krim had cost some delay, but Hoddan arrived back at a positive sight of Darth's sun within a day or so. Then there was little or no time lost in getting into orbit with the junk yard spacefleet of the emigrants. Shortly thereafter he called the leader's ship with only mild worries about possible disasters that might have happened while he was away.

"Calling the leader's ship," he said crisply. "Calling the leader's ship! This is Bron Hoddan, reporting back from Walden with a ship and machinery contributed for your use!"

The harsh voice of the bearded old leader of the emigrants seemed somehow broken when he replied. He called down blessings on Hoddan, who could use them. Then there was the matter of getting the emigrants on board the new ship. They didn't know how to use the lifeboat tubes. Hoddan had to demonstrate. But shortly after, there were twenty, thirty, fifty of the folk from Colin, feverishly searching the ship and incredulously reporting what they found.

"It's impossible!" said the old man. "It's impossible!"

"I wouldn't say that," said Hoddan. "It's unlikely, but it's happened. I'm only afraid it's not enough."

"It is many times more than what we hoped," said the old man humbly. "Only—he stopped. "We are more grateful than we can say."

Hoddan took a deep breath.

"I'd like to take my crew back home," he explained. "And come back. Perhaps I can be useful explaining things. And I'd like to ask a great favor of you—for my own work."

"But naturally," said the old man. "Of course. We will await your return."

Hoddan was relieved. There seemed to be a strange limitation to the happiness of the emigrants. They were passionately rejoiceful over the agricultural machinery. But they seemed dutifully rather than truly happy over the microfilm library. The vision-tape instructors were the objects of polite comment only. Hoddan felt a vague discomfort. There seemed to be a sort of secret desperation in the atmosphere, which they would not admit or mention. But he was coming back. Of course.

He brought the spaceboat over to the new liner. He hooked onto a lifeboat blister and his seven Darthians crawled through the lifeboat tube. Hoddan pulled away quickly before somebody thought to ask why there were no lifeboats in the places so plainly made for them.

He headed downward when the landmarks on Darth's surface told him that Don Loris' castle would shortly come over the horizon. He was just touching atmosphere when it did. The boat's tanks had been refilled, and he burned fuel recklessly to make a dramatic landing within a hundred yards of the battlements where Fani had once thoughtfully had a coil of rope ready for him.

Heads peered at the lifeboat over those same battlements now, but the gate was closed. It stayed closed. There was somehow an atmosphere of suspicion amounting to enmity. Hoddan felt unwelcome.

"All right, boys," he said resignedly. "Out with you and to the castle. Here's your loot from the voyage." He counted out for each of them rather more actual cash than any of them really believed in. "And I want you to take this box to Don Loris. It's a gift from me. And I want to consult with him about co-operation between the two of us in some plans I have. Ask if I may come and talk to him."

His seven former spearmen tumbled out. They marched gleefully to the castle gate. Hoddan saw them make a tantalizing display of the large sums of cash to the watchers above them. Thal held up the box for Don Loris. It was the box the lawyer's clerk had turned over to him, with a tidy sum in cash in it. The sum was partly depleted, now. Hoddan had paid off his involuntary crew with it. But there was still more in it than Don Loris would have gotten from Walden for selling him out.

The castle gate opened, as if grudgingly. The seven went in.

Time passed. Much time. Hoddan went over the arguments he meant to use on Don Loris. He needed to make up a very great sum, and it could be done thus-and-so, but thus-and-so required occasional pirate raids, which called for crews, and if Don Loris would encourage his retainers… He could have gone to another Darthian chieftain, of course, but he knew what kind of scoundrel Don Loris was. He'd have to find out about another man.

Nearly an hour elapsed before the castle gate opened again. Two files of spearmen marched out. There were eight men with a sergeant in command. Hoddan did not recognize any of them. They came to the spaceboat. The sergeant formally presented an official message. Don Loris would admit Bron Hoddan to his presence, to hear what he had to say.

Hoddan felt excessively uncomfortable. Waiting, he'd thought about that secret despair in the emigrant fleet. He worried about it. He was concerned because Don Loris had not welcomed him with cordiality, now that he'd brought back his retainers in good working order. In a sudden gloomy premonition, he checked his stun-pistols. They needed charging. He managed it from the life-boat unit.

He went with foreboding toward the castle with the eight spearmen surrounding him as cops had once surrounded him on Walden. He did not like to be reminded of it. He frowned to himself as he went in the castle gate, and along a long stone passage, and up stone stairs into the great hall of state. Don Loris, as once before, sat peevishly by the huge fireplace. This time he was almost inside it, with its hood and mantel actually over his head. The Lady Fani sat there with him.

Don Loris seemed to put aside his peevishness only a little to greet Hoddan.

"My dear fellow," he said complainingly, "I don't like to welcome you with reproaches, but do you know that when you absconded with that spaceboat, you made a mortal enemy for me? It's a fact! My neighbor, on whose land the boat descended, was deeply hurt. He considered it his property. He had summoned his retainers for a fight over it when I heard of his resentment and partly soothed him with apologies and presents. But he still considers that I should return it to him, whenever you appear here with it!"

"Oh," said Hoddan. "That's too bad."

Things looked ominous. The Lady Fani looked at him strangely. As if she were trying to tell him something without speaking. She looked as if she had wept lately.

"To be sure," said Don Loris fretfully, "to be sure you gave me a very pretty present just now. But my retainers tell me that you came back with a ship. A very fine ship. What became of it? The landing-grid has been repaired at last and you could have landed there. What happened to it?"

"I gave it away," said Hoddan. He saw what Fani was trying to tell him. Leading into the great hall was a corridor filled with spearmen. His tone turned sardonic. "I gave it to a poor old man."

Don Loris shook his head.

"That's not right, Hoddan! That fleet overhead, now. If they are pirates and want some of my men for crews, they should come to me! I don't take kindly to the idea of your kidnapping my men and carrying them off on piratical excursions! They must be profitable! But on the other hand, if you can afford to give me presents like this, and be so lavish with my retainers—why maybe…"

Hoddan grimaced.

"I came to arrange a deal on that order," he observed.

"I don't think I like it," said Don Loris peevishly. "I prefer to deal with people direct. I'll arrange about the landing-grid, and for a regular recruiting service which I will conduct, of course. But you—you are irresponsible! I wish you well, but when you carry my men off for pirates, and make my neighbor's into my enemies, and infect my daughter with strange notions and the government of a friendly planet asks me in so many words not to shelter you any longer—why, that's the end, Hoddan. So with great regret…"

"The regret is mine," said Hoddan. Thoughtfully, he aimed a stun-pistol at a slowly opening corridor door. He pulled the trigger. Yells followed its humming, because not everybody it hit was knocked out. Nor did it hit everybody in the corridor. Men came surging out of one door, and then two.

Then a spear went past Hoddan's face and missed him only by inches. It buried its point in the floor. A whirling knife spun past his nose. He glanced up. There were balconies all around the great hall, and men popped up from behind the railings and threw things at him. They popped down out of sight instantly. There was no rhythm involved. He could not anticipate their rising, nor shoot them through the balcony-front. And more men infiltrated the hall, getting behind heavy chairs and tables. More spears and knives flew.

"Bron!" cried the Lady Fani, throatily.

He thought she had an exit for him. He sprang to her side.

"I—I didn't want you to come," she wept.

There was a singular pause in the clangings and clashings of weapons on the floor. Then one man popped up and hurled a knife. The clang of its fall was a very lonely one. Don Loris fairly howled at him.

"Idiot! Think of the Lady Fani!"

The Lady Fani suddenly smiled tremulously.

"Wonderful!" she said. "They don't dare do anything while you're as close to me as this!"

"Do you suppose," asked Hoddan, "I could count on that?"

"I'm certain of it!" said Fani. "And I think you'd better."

"Then, excuse me," said Hoddan with great politeness.

He swung her up and over his shoulder. With a stun-pistol in his free hand he headed down the hall.

"Outside," she said zestfully, "get out the side door and turn left, and nobody can jump down on your neck. Then left again to the gate."

He obeyed. Now and again he got in a pot-shot with his pistol. Don Loris had turned the castle into a very pretty trap. The Lady Fani said plaintively:

"This is terribly undignified, and I can't see where we're going. Where are we now?"

"Almost at the gate," panted Hoddan. "At it, now." He swung out of the massive entrance to Don Loris' stronghold. "I'll put you down now."

"I wouldn't," said the Lady Fani. "I think you'd better make for the spaceboat exactly as we are."

Again Hoddan obeyed, racing across the open ground. Howls of fury followed him. It was evidently the opinion of the castle that the Lady Fani was to be abducted in the place of the seven returned spearmen.

Hoddan, breathing hard, reached the spaceboat. He put Fani down and said anxiously:

"You're all right? I'm very much in your debt! I was in a spot!" Then he nodded toward the castle. "They're upset, aren't they? They must think I mean to kidnap you."

The Lady Fani beamed.

"It would be terrible if you did," she said hopefully. "I couldn't do a thing to stop you! And a successful public abduction's a legal marriage, on Darth! Wouldn't it be terrible?"

Hoddan mopped his face and patted her reassuringly on the shoulder.

"Don't worry!" he said warmly. "You just got me out of an awful fix! You're my friend! And anyhow I'm going to marry a girl on Walden, named Nedda. Goodbye, Fani! Keep clear of the rocket blast."

He went into the boat's port, turned to smile paternally back at her, and shut the port behind him. Seconds later the spaceboat took off. It left behind clouds of rocket smoke.

And, though Hoddan hadn't the faintest idea of it, he had left behind the maddest girl in several solar systems.

# CHAPTER X

It is the custom of all men, everywhere, to be obtuse where women are concerned: Hoddan went skyward in the spaceboat with feelings of warm gratitude toward the Lady Fani. He had not the slightest inkling that she, had anything but the friendliest of feelings toward him.

As Hoddan drove on up and up, the sky became deep purple and then black velvet set with flecks of fire. He was relieved by the welcome he'd received earlier today from the emigrants, but he remained slightly puzzled by a very faint impression of desperation remaining. He felt very virtuous on the whole, however, and his plans for the future were specific. He'd already composed a letter to his grandfather, which he'd ask the emigrant fleet to deliver. He had another letter in his mind, a form letter—practically a public-relations circular—which he hoped to whip into shape before the emigrants got too anxious to be on their way. He considered that he needed to earn a little more of their gratitude so he could make everything come out even; everybody being satisfied and happy but himself.

For himself he anticipated only the deep satisfaction of accomplishment. He'd wanted to do great things since he was a small boy. He'd gone to Walden in the hope of achievement. There, of course, he failed because in a free economy, industrialists consider that freedom is the privilege of being stupid without penalty. But Hoddan now believed himself in the fascinating situation of having knowledge and abilities which were needed by other people.

It was only when he'd made contact with the fleet, and was in the act of maneuvering toward a boat-blister on the liner he'd brought back, that doubts again assailed him. He had done a few things—accomplished little. He'd devised a broadcast-power receptor and a microwave projector and he'd turned a Lawlor drive into a ball-lightning projector and worked out a few little things like that. But the first had been invented before by somebody in the Cetis cluster, and the second could have been made by anybody and the third was standard practice on Zan. He still had to do something significant.

When he made fast to the liner and crawled through the tube to its hull, he was in a state of doubt which passed very well for modesty.

The bearded old man received him in the skipper's quarters, which Hoddan himself had occupied for a few days. He looked very weary. He seemed to have aged, in hours.

"We grow more astounded by the minute," he told Hoddan heavily, "by what you have brought us. Ten shiploads like this and we would be better equipped than we believed ourselves in the beginning. It looks as if some thousands of us will now be able to survive our colonization of the planet Thetis."

Hoddan gaped at him. The old man put his hand on Hoddan's shoulder.

"We are grateful," he said with a pathetic attempt at warmth. "Please do not doubt that! It is only that…that…I cannot help wishing very desperately that…that instead of unfamiliar tools for metal-working and machines with tapes which show pictures—I wish that even one more jungle plow had been included!"

Hoddan's jaw dropped. The people of Colin wanted planet-subduing machinery. They wanted it so badly that they did not want anything else. They could not even see that anything else had any value at all. Most of them could only look forward to starvation when the ships' supplies were exhausted, because not enough ground could be broken and cultivated early enough to grow food enough in time.

"Would it," asked the old man desperately, "would it be possible to exchange these useless machines for others that will be useful?"

"Let me talk to your mechanics, sir," said Hoddan unhappily. "Maybe something can be done."

He restrained himself from tearing his hair as he went to where the mechanics of the fleet looked over their new equipment. He'd come up to the fleet again to gloat and do great things for people who needed him and knew it. But he faced the hopelessness of people to whom his utmost effort seemed mockery because it was so far from being enough.

He gathered together the men who'd tried to keep the fleet's ships in working order during their flight. They were competent men, of course. They were resolute. But now they had given up hope. Hoddan began to lecture them. They needed machines. He hadn't brought the machines they wanted, perhaps, but he'd brought the machines to make them with. Here were automatic shapers, turret lathes, dicers. He'd brought these because they already had the raw material—the ships themselves! Even some of the junk they carried in crates was good metal, merely worn out in its present form. They could make anything they needed with what he'd brought them. For example, he'd show them how to make a lumber saw.

He showed them how to make the slender, rapier-like revolving tool with which a man stabbed a tree and cut outward with the speed of a hot knife cutting butter. And one could mount it so, and cut out planks and beams for temporary bridges and such constructions.

They watched, baffled. They gave no sign of hope. They did not want lumber saws. They wanted jungle-breaking machinery.

"I've brought you everything!" he insisted. "You've got a civilization, compact, on this ship! You've got life instead of starvation! Look at this. I'll make a water pump to irrigate your fields!"

Before their eyes he turned out an irrigation pump on an automatic shaper. He showed them that the shaper went on, by itself, making other pumps without further instructions.

The mechanics stirred uneasily. They had watched without comprehension. Now they listened without enthusiasm. Their eyes were like those of children who watch marvels without comprehension.

He made a sledge whose runners slid on the air between themselves and whatever object would otherwise have touched them. It was practically frictionless. He made a machine to make nails. He made a power-hammer which hummed and pushed nails into any object that needed to be nailed. He made—He stopped abruptly, and sat down with his head in his hands. The people of the fleet faced so overwhelming a catastrophe that they could not see through it. They could only experience it. As their leader would have been unable to answer questions about the fleet's predicament before he'd poured out the tale in the form it had taken in his mind, now these mechanics were unable to see ahead. They were paralyzed by the completeness of the disaster before them. They could live until the supplies of the fleet gave out. They could not grow fresh supplies without jungle-breaking machinery. They had to have jungle-breaking machinery. They could not imagine wanting anything more or less than jungle-breaking machinery.

Hoddan raised his head. The mechanics looked dully at him.

"You men do maintenance?" he asked. "You repair things when they wear out on the ships? Have you run out of some of the materials you need for repairs?"

After a long time a tired-looking man said slowly:

"On the ship I come from, were having trouble. Our hydroponic garden keeps the air fresh, o' course. But the water-circulation pipes are gone. Rusted through. We haven't got any pipe to fix them with. We have to keep the water moving with buckets."

Hoddan got up. He looked about him. He hadn't brought hydroponic piping. And there was no raw material. He took a pair of power-snips and cut away a section of wall lining. He cut it into strips. He asked the diameter of the pipe. Before their eyes he made pipe—spirally wound around a mandrel and line-welded to solidity.

"I need some of that on my ship," said another man.

The bearded man said heavily:

"We'll make some and send it to the ships that need it."

"No," said Hoddan. "We'll send the tools to make it. We can make the tools here. There must be other kinds of repairs, too. With the machines I've brought, we'll make the tools to make repairs. Picture-tape machines have reels that show exactly how to do it."

It was a new idea. The mechanics had other and immediate problems beside the over-all disaster of the fleet. Pumps that did not work. Motors that heated up. They could envision the meeting of those problems, and they could envision the obtaining of jungle plows. But they couldn't imagine anything in between. They were capable of learning how to make tools for repairs.

Hoddan taught them. In one day there were five ships being brought into better operating condition—for ultimate futility—because of what he'd brought. Two days. Three. Mechanics began to come to the liner. Those who'd learned first, pompously passed on what they knew. On the fourth day somebody began to use a vision-tape machine to get information on a fine point in welding. On the fifth day there were lines of men waiting to use them.

On the sixth day a mechanic on what had been a luxury passenger liner scores of years ago, asked to talk to Hoddan by space-phone. He'd been working feverishly at the minor repairs he'd been unable to make for so long. To get material he pulled a crate off one of the junk machines supplied the fleet. He looked it over. He believed that if this piece were made new, and that replaced with sound metal, the machine might be usable!

Hoddan had him come to the liner which was now the flagship of the fleet. Discussion began and Hoddan began to draw diagrams. They were not clear. He drew more. Abruptly, he stared at what he'd outlined. He saw something remarkable. If one applied a perfectly well-known bit of pure-science information that nobody bothered with... He finished the diagram and a vast, soothing satisfaction came over him.

"We've got to get out of here!" he said. "Not enough room!"

He looked about him. Insensibly, as he talked to the first man on the fleet to show imagination, other men had gathered around. They were now absorbed.

"I think," said Hoddan, "that we can make an electronic field that'll soften the cementite between the crystals of steel, without heating up anything else. If it works, we can use plastic dies! And then that useless junk you've got can be rebuilt."

They listened gravely, nodding as he talked. They did not quite understand everything, but they had the habit of believing him now.

Soon Hoddan had a cold-metal die-stamper in operation. It was very large. It drew on the big ship's drive-unit for power.

One put a rough mass of steel in place between plastic dies. One turned on the power. In a tenth of a second the steel was soft as putty. Then it stiffened and was warm. But in that tenth of a second it had been shaped with precision.

It took two days to duplicate the jungle plow Hoddan had first been shown, in new, sound metal. But after the first one worked triumphantly, they made forty of each part at a time and turned out enough jungle plows for the subjugation of all Thetis' forests.

One day Hoddan waked from a cat nap with a diagram in his head. He drew it, half-asleep, and later looked and found that his unconscious mind had designed a power-supply system which made Walden's look rather primitive.

During the first six days Hoddan did not sleep to speak of, and after that he merely cat-napped when he could. But he finally agreed with the emigrants' leader—now no longer fierce, but fiercely triumphant—that he thought they could go on. And he would ask a favor. He propped his eyelids open with his fingers and wrote the letter to his grandfather that he'd composed in his mind in the liner on Krim. He managed to make one copy, unaddressed, of the public-relations letter that he'd worked out at the same time. He put it through a facsimile machine and managed to address each of fifty copies. Then he yawned uncontrollably.

He still yawned when he went to take leave of the leader of the people of Colin. That person regarded him with warm eyes.

"I think everything's all right," said Hoddan exhaustedly. "You've got a dozen machine-shops and they're multiplying themselves, and you've got some enthusiastic mechanics, now, who're drinking in the vision-tape stuff and finding out more than they guessed there ever was. And they're thinking, now and then, for themselves. I think you'll make out."

The bearded man said humbly:

"I have waited until you said all was well. Will you come with us?"

"No-o-o," said Hoddan. He yawned again. "I've got my work here. There's an obligation I have to meet."

"It must be very admirable work," said the old man wistfully. "I wish we had some young men like you among us."

"You have," said Hoddan. "They'll be giving you trouble presently."

The old man shook his head, looking at Hoddan very affectionately.

"We will deliver your letters," he said warmly. "First to Krim, and then to Walden. Then we will go on and let down your letter and gift to your grandfather on Zan. Then we will go on toward Thetis. Our mechanics will work at building machines while we are in overdrive. But also they will build new tool shops and train new mechanics, so that every so often we will need to come out of overdrive to transfer the tools and the men to new ships."

Hoddan nodded exhaustedly. This was right.

"So," said the old man contentedly, "we will simply make those transfers in orbit about the planets for which we have your letters. You will pardon us if we only let down your letters, and do not visit those planets? We have prejudices."

"Perfectly satisfactory," said Hoddan.

"The mechanics you have trained," said the old man proudly, "have made a little ship ready for you. It is not much larger than your spaceboat, but it is fit for travel between suns, which will be convenient for your work. I hope you will accept it. There is even a tiny tool shop on it!"

Hoddan would have been more touched if he hadn't known about it. But one of the men entrusted with the job had needed his advice. He knew what he was getting. It was the spaceyacht he'd used before, refurbished and fitted with everything the emigrants could provide.

He affected great surprise and expressed unfeigned appreciation. Barely an hour later he transferred to it with the spaceboat in tow. He watched the emigrant fleet swing out to emptiness and resume its valiant journey. But it was not a hopeless journey, now. In fact, the colony on Thetis ought to start out better equipped than most settled planets.

And he went to sleep. He'd nothing urgent to do, except allow a certain amount of time pass before he did anything. He was exhausted. He slept the clock round, and waked and ate sluggishly, and went back to sleep again. On the whole, the cosmos did not notice the difference. Stars flamed in emptiness, and planets rotated sedately. Comets flung out gossamer veils or retracted them, and spaceliners went about upon their lawful occasions.

When he waked again he was rested, and he reviewed all his actions and his situation. It appeared that matters promised fairly well on the emigrant fleet now gone forever. They would remember Hoddan with affection for a year or so, and dimly after that. But settling a new world would be enthralling and important work. Nobody'd think of him at all, after a certain length of time. But he had to think of an obligation he'd assumed on their account.

He considered his own affairs. He'd told Fani he was going to marry Nedda. The way things looked, that was no longer so probable. Of course, in a year or two, or a few years, he might be out from under the obligations he now considered due. In time even the Waldenian government would realize that death rays didn't exist, and a lawyer might be able to clear things for his return to Walden. But Nedda was a nice girl…

He frowned. That was it. She was a remarkably nice girl. But Hoddan suddenly doubted if she were a delightful one. He found himself questioning that she was exactly and perfectly what his long-cherished ambitions described. He tried to imagine spending his declining years with Nedda. He couldn't quite picture it as exciting. She did tend to be a little insipid.

Presently, gloomy and a trifle dogged about it, he brought the spaceboat around to the modernized boat-port of the yacht. He got into it, leaving the yacht in orbit. He headed down toward Darth. Now that he'd rested, he had work to do which could not be neglected. To carry out that work, he needed a crew able and willing to pass for pirates for a pirate's pay. And there were innumerable castles on Darth, with quite as many shifty noblemen, and certainly no fewer plunder-hungry Darthian gentlemen hanging around them. But Don Loris' castle had one real advantage and one which existed only in Hoddan's mind.

Don Loris' retainers knew that Hoddan had led their companions to loot. Large loot. He'd have less trouble and more enthusiastic support from Don Loris' retainers than any other. This was true.

The illusion was that the Lady Fani was his firm personal friend with no nonsense about her. This was a very great mistake.

He landed for the fourth time outside Don Loris' castle. This time he had no booty-laden men to march to the castle and act as heralds of his presence. The spaceboat's vision screens showed Don Loris' stronghold as squat, immense, dark and menacing. Banners flew from its turrets, their colors bright in the ruddy light of near-sunset. The gate remained closed. For a long time there was no sign that his landing had been noted. Then there was movement on the battlements, and a figure began to descend outside the wall. It was lowered to the ground by a long rope.

It reached the ground and shook itself. It marched toward the spaceboat through the red and nearly level rays of the dying sun. Hoddan watched with a frown on his face. This wasn't a retainer of Don Loris'. It assuredly wasn't Fani. He couldn't even make out its gender until the figure was very near.

Then he looked astonished. It was his old friend Derec, arrived on Darth a long while since in the spaceboat Hoddan had been using ever since. Derec had been his boon companion in the days when he expected to become rich by splendid exploits in electronics. Derec was also the character who'd conscientiously told the cops on Hoddan, when they found his power-receptor sneaked into a Mid-Continent station and a stray corpse coincidentally outside.

He opened the boat-port and stood in the opening. Derec had been a guest in Don Loris' castle for a good long while, now. Hoddan wondered if he considered his quarters cozy.

"Evening, Derec," said Hoddan cordially. "You're looking well!"

"I don't feel it," said Derec dismally. "I feel like a fool in the castle yonder. And the high police official I came here with has gotten grumpy and snaps when I try to speak to him."

Hoddan said gravely:

"I'm sure the Lady Fani—"

"A tigress!" said Derec bitterly: "We don't get along."

Looking at Derec, Hoddan found himself able to understand why. Derec was the sort of friend one might make on Walden for lack of something better. He was well-meaning. He might even be capable of splendid things—even heroism. But he was horribly, terribly, appallingly civilized!

"Well! Well!" said Hoddan kindly. "And what's on your mind, Derec?"

"I came," said Derec dismally, "to plead with you again, Bron. You must surrender! There's nothing else to do! People can't have death rays, Bron! Above all, you mustn't tell the pirates how to make them!"

Hoddan was puzzled for a moment. Then he realized that Derec's information about the fleet came from the spearmen he'd brought back, loaded down with cash. Derec hadn't noticed the absence of the flashing lights at sunset—or hadn't realized that they meant the fleet had gone away.

"Hm," said Hoddan. "Why don't you think I've already done it?"

"Because they'd have killed you," said Derec. "Don Loris pointed that out. He doesn't believe you know how to make death rays. He says it's not a secret anybody would be willing for anybody else to know. But you know the truth, Bron! You killed that poor man back on Walden. You've got to sacrifice yourself for humanity! You'll be treated kindly!"

Hoddan shook his head. It seemed somehow very startling for Derec to be harping on that same idea, after so many things had happened to Hoddan. But he didn't think Derec would actually expect him to yield to persuasion. There must be something else. Derec might even have nerved himself up to do something quite desperate.

"What did you really come here for, Derec?"

"To beg you to—"

Then, in one instant, Derec made a hysterical gesture and Hoddan's stun-pistol hummed. A small object left Derec's hand as his muscles convulsed from the stun-pistol bolt. It did not fly quite true. It fell a foot or so to one side of the boat-port instead of inside.

It exploded luridly as Derec crumpled. There was thick, strangling smoke. Hoddan disappeared. When the thickest smoke drifted away there was nothing to be seen but Derec lying on the ground, and thinner smoke drifting out of the still-open boat-port.

Nearly half an hour later, figures came very cautiously toward the spaceboat. Thal was their leader. His expression was mournful and depressed. Other brawny retainers came uncertainly behind him. At a nod from Thal, two of them picked up Derec and carted him off toward the castle.

"I guess he got it," said Thal dismally. He peered in. He shook his head. "Wounded, maybe, and crawled off to die." He peered in again and shook his head once more. "No sign of 'im."

A spearman just behind Thal said:

"Dirty trick! I was with him to Walden, and he paid off good! A good man! Shoulda been a chieftain! Good man!"

Thal gingerly entered the spaceboat. He wrinkled his nose at the faint smell of explosive still inside. Another man came in. Another.

"Say!" said one of them in a conspiratorial voice. "We got our share of that loot from Walden. But he hadda share, too! What'd he do with it? He could've kept it in this boat here. We could take a quick look! What Don Loris don't know don't hurt him!"

"I'm going to find Hoddan first," said Thal, with dignity. "We don't have to carry him outside so's Don Loris knows we're looking for loot, but I'm going to find him first."

There were other men in the spaceboat now. A full dozen of them. Their spears were very much in the way.

The boat-door closed quietly. Don Loris' retainers stared at each other. The locking-dogs grumbled for half a second, sealing the door tightly. Don Loris' retainers began to babble protestingly.

There was a roaring outside. The spaceboat stirred. The roaring rose to thunder. The boat lurched. It flung the spearmen into a sprawling, swearing, terrified heap at the rear end of the boat's interior.

The boat went on out to space again. In the control-room Hoddan said dourly to himself:

"I'm in a rut. I've got to figure out some way to ship a pirate crew without having to kidnap them. This is getting monotonous!"

# CHAPTER XI

There was a disturbed air which enveloped all the members of Hoddan's crew, on the way to Walden. It was not exactly reluctance, because there was self-evident enthusiasm over the idea of making a pirate voyage under him. When men went off with Hoddan, they came back rich.

But nevertheless there was an uncomfortable sort of atmosphere in the renovated yacht. They'd transshipped from the spaceboat to the yacht through lifeboat-tubes, and they were quite docile about it because none of them knew how to get back to ground. Hoddan left the spaceboat with a timing signal set for use on his return. He'd done a similar thing off Krim. He drove the little yacht well out, until Darth was only a spotted ball with visible clouds and icecaps. Then he lined up for Walden, direct, and went into overdrive.

Within hours he noted the disturbing feel of things. His followers were not happy. They moped. They sat in corners and submerged themselves in misery. Large, massive men with drooping blonde moustaches—ideal characters for the roles of pirates—had tears rolling down from their eyes at odd moments. When the ship was twelve hours on its way, the atmosphere inside it was funereal. The spearmen did not even gorge themselves on the food with which the yacht was stocked. And when a Darthian gentleman lost his appetite, something had to be wrong.

He called Thal into the control-room.

"What's the matter with the gang?" he demanded vexedly. "They look at me as if I'd broken all their hearts! Do they want to go back?"

Thal heaved a sigh, indicating depression beside which suicidal mania would be hilarity. He said pathetically:

"We cannot go back. We cannot ever return to Darth. We are lost men, doomed to wander forever among strangers, or to float as corpses between the stars."

"What happened?" demanded Hoddan. "I'm taking you on a pirate cruise where the loot should be a lot better than last time!"

Thal wept. Hoddan astonishedly regarded his whiskery countenance, contorted with grief and dampened with tears.

"It happened at the castle," said Thal miserably. "The man Derec, from Walden, had thrown a bomb at you. You seemed to be dead. But Don Loris was not sure. He fretted, as he does. He wished to send someone to make sure. The Lady Fani said: 'I will make sure!' She called me to her and said, 'Thal, will you fight for me?' And there was Don Loris suddenly nodding beside her. So I said, 'Yes, my Lady Fani.' Then she said: 'Thank you. I am troubled by Bron Hoddan.' So what could I do? She said the same thing to each of us, and each of us had to say that he would fight for her. To each she said that she was troubled by you. Then Don Loris sent us out to look at your body. And now we are disgraced!"

Hoddan's mouth opened and closed and opened again. He remembered this item of Darthian etiquette. If a girl asked a man if he would fight for her, and he agreed, then within a day and a night he had to fight the man she sent him to fight, or else he was disgraced. And disgrace on Darth meant that the shamed man could be plundered or killed by anybody who chose to do so—and he would be hanged by indignant authority if he resisted. It was a great deal worse than outlawry. It included scorn and contempt and opprobrium. It meant dishonor and humiliation and admitted degradation. A disgraced man was despicable in his own eyes. And Hoddan had kidnapped these men who'd been forced to engage themselves to fight him, and if they killed him they would obviously die in space, and if they didn't they'd be ashamed to stay alive. The moral tone on Darth was probably not elevated, but etiquette was a force.

Hoddan thought it over. He looked up suddenly.

"Some of them," he said wryly, "probably figure there's nothing to do but go through with it, eh?"

"Yes," said Thal dismally. "Then we will all die."

"Hmm," said Hoddan. "The obligation is to fight. If you fail to kill me, that's not your fault, is it? If you're conquered you're in the clear?"

"True. Too true!" Thal said miserably. "When a man is conquered he is conquered. His conqueror may plunder him, when the matter is finished, or he can spare him, then he may never fight his conqueror again."

"Draw your knife," said Hoddan. "Come at me."

Thal made a bewildered gesture. Hoddan leveled a stun-pistol and said:

"Bzzz. You're conquered. You came at me with your knife, and I shot you with my stun-pistol. It's all over. Right?"

Thal gaped at him. Then he beamed. He expanded. He gloated. He frisked. He practically wagged a non-existent tail in his exuberance. He'd been shown an out when he could see none.

"Send in the others one by one," said Hoddan. "I'll take care of them. But Thal, why did the Lady Fani want me killed?"

Thal had no idea, but he did not care. Hoddan did care. He was bewildered and inclined to be indignant. A noble friendship like theirs—A spearman came in and saluted. Hoddan went through a symbolic duel, which was plainly the way the thing would have happened in reality. Others came in and went through the same process. Two of them did not quite grasp that it was a ritual, and he had to shoot them in the knife-arm. Then he hunted in the ship's supplies for ointment for the blisters that would appear from stun-pistol bolts at such short range. As he bandaged the places, he again tried to find out why the Lady Fani had tried to get him carved up. Nobody could enlighten him.

But the atmosphere improved remarkably. Since each theoretic fight had taken place in private, nobody was obliged to admit a compromise with etiquette. Hoddan's followers ceased to brood. They developed huge appetites. Those who had been aground on Krim told zestfully of the monstrous hangovers they'd acquired there. It appeared that Hoddan was revered for the size of the benders he enabled his followers to hang on.

But there remained the fact that the Lady Fani had tried to get him massacred. He puzzled over it. The little yacht sped through space toward Walden. He tried to think how he'd offended Fani.

He could think of nothing. He set to work on a new electronic set-up which would make still another modification of the Lawlor space-drive possible. In the others, groups of electronic components were cut out and others substituted in rather tricky fashion from the control board. This was trickiest of all. It required the homemade vacuum tube to burn steadily when in use. But it was a very simple idea. Lawlor drive and landing-grid forcefields were formed by not dissimilar generators, and ball-lightning forcefields were in the same general family of phenomena. Suppose one made the field generator that had to be on a ship if it were to drive at all, capable of all those allied, associated, similar forcefields? If a ship could make the fields that landing-grids did, it should be useful to pirates.

Hoddan's present errand was neither pure nor simple piracy, but piracy it would be. The more he considered the obligation he'd taken on himself when he helped the emigrants, the more he doubted that he could lift it without long struggle. He was preparing to carry on that struggle for a long time. He'd more or less resigned himself to the postponement of his personal desires—Nedda, for example.

But time passed, and he finished his electronic job. He came out of overdrive and made his observations and corrected his course. Finally, there came a moment when the fiery ball which was Walden's sun shone brightly in the vision-plates. It writhed and spun in the vast silence of emptiness.

Hoddan drove to a point still above the five-diameter limit of Walden. He interestedly switched on the control which made his drive-unit manufacture landing-grid type forcefields. He groped for Walden, and felt the peculiar rigidity of the ship when the field took hold somewhere underground. He made an adjustment, and felt the ship respond. Instead of pulling a ship to ground, in the set-up he'd made, the new fields pulled the ground toward the ship. When he reversed the adjustment, instead of pushing the ship away to empty space, the new field pushed the planet.

There was no practical difference, of course. The effect was simply that the spaceyacht now carried its own landing-grid. It could descend anywhere and ascend from anywhere without using rockets. Moreover, it could hover without using power.

Hoddan was pleased. He took the yacht down to a bare four hundred-mile altitude. He stopped it there. It was highly satisfactory. He made quite certain that everything worked as it should. Then he made a call on the space-communicator.

"Calling ground," said Hoddan. "Calling ground. Pirate ship calling ground!"

He waited for an answer. Now he'd set the results of his efforts and planning. He was apprehensive, of course. There was much responsibility on his shoulders. There was the liner he'd captured and looted and given to the emigrants. There were his followers on the yacht, now enthusiastically sharpening their two-foot knives in expectation of loot. He owed these people something. For an instant he thought of the Lady Fani and wondered how he could make reparation to her for whatever had hurt her feelings.

A whining, bitterly unhappy voice came to him.

"Pirate ship!" said the voice plaintively, "we received the fleet's warning. Please state where you intend to descend. We will take measures to prevent disorder. Repeat, please state where you intend to descend and we will take measures to prevent disorder."

Hoddan drew a sharp breath of relief. He named a spot—a high-income, residential small city, some forty miles from the planetary capitol. He set his controls for a very gradual descent. He went out to where his followers made grisly zinging noises where they honed their knives.

"We'll land," said Hoddan sternly, "in about three-quarters of an hour. You will go ashore and loot in parties of not less than three! Thal, you will be ship-guard and receive the plunder and make sure that nobody from Walden gets on board. You will not waste time committing atrocities on the population!"

He went back to the control-room. He turned to general communication bands and listened to the broadcasts down below.

"Special Emergency Bulletin!" boomed a voice. "Pirates are landing in the city of Ensfield, forty miles from Walden City. The population is instructed to evacuate immediately, leaving all action to the police. Repeat! The population will evacuate Ensfield, leaving all action to the police. Take nothing with you. Take nothing with you. Leave at once."

Hoddan nodded approvingly. The voice boomed again:

"Special Emergency Bulletin! Pirates are landing. Evacuate. Take nothing with you. Leave at once."

He turned to another channel. An excited voice barked:

"Seems to be only the one pirate ship, which has been located hovering in an unknown manner over Ensfield. We are rushing cameramen to the spot and will try to give on-the-spot, as-it-happens coverage of the landing of pirates on Walden, their looting of the city of Ensfield, and the traffic jams inevitable in the departure of the citizens before the pirate ship touches ground. For background information on this the most exciting event in planetary history, I take you to our editorial rooms." Another voice took over instantly. "It will be remembered that some days since the gigantic pirate fleet then overhead sent down a communication to the planetary government, warning that single ships would appear to loot and giving notice that any resistance—"

Hoddan felt a contented, heart-warming glow. The emigrant fleet had most faithfully carried out its leader's promise to let down a letter from space while in orbit around Walden. The emigrants, of course, did not know the contents of the letter. Blithely, cheerfully, and dutifully, they gave the appearance of monstrous piratical strength. They had awed Walden thoroughly. And then they'd gone on, faithfully leaving similar letters and similar impressions on Krim, Lohala, Tralee, Famagusta, and all throughout the Coalsack stars until the stock of addressed missives ran out. They would perform this kindly act out of gratitude to Hoddan.

And every planet they visited would be left with the impression that the fleet overhead was that of bloodthirsty space-marauders who would presently send single ships to collect loot, which must be yielded without resistance. Such looting expeditions were to be looked for regularly and must be submitted to under penalty of unthinkable retribution from the monster fleet of space.

Now, as the yacht descended on Walden, it represented that mythical but impressive piratical empire. He listened with genuine pleasure to the broadcasts. When low enough, he even picked up the pictures of highways thronged with fugitives from the to-be-looted town. He saw Waldenian police directing the traffic of flight. He saw other traffic heading toward the city. Walden was the most highly civilized planet in the Nurmi Cluster, and its citizens had had no worries at all except about the tranquilizers to enable them to stand it. When something genuinely exciting turned up, they wanted to be there to see it.

The yacht descended below the clouds. Hoddan turned on an emergency flare to make a landing by. Sitting in the control-room he saw his own ship as the broadcast-cameras picked it up and relayed it to millions of homes. He was impressed. It was a glaring eye of fierce light, descending deliberately with a dark and mysterious spacecraft behind it. He heard the chattered, on-the-spot-news accounts of the happening. He saw the people who had not left Ensfield joined by avid visitors. He saw all of them held back by police, who frantically shepherded them away from the area in which the pirates should begin their horrid work.

Hoddan even watched pleasurably from his control-room as the cameras daringly showed the actual touch-down of the ship: the dramatic slow opening of its port: the appearance of authentic pirates in the opening, armed to the teeth, bristling ferociously, glaring about them at the silent, deserted streets of the city left to their mercy.

It was a splendid broadcast. Hoddan would liked to have stayed and watched all of it. But he had work to do. He had to supervise the pirate raid.

It was, as it turned out, simple enough. Looting parties of three pirates each, moved skulking about, seeking plunder. Quaking cameramen dared to ask them, in shaking voices, to pose for the news cameras. It was a request no Darthian gentleman, even in an act of piracy, could possibly refuse. They posed, making pictures of malignant ruffianism.

Commentators, adding informed comment to delectably thrilling pictures, observed that the pirates wore Darthian costume, but observed crisply that this did not mean that Darth as an entity had turned pirate, but only that some of her citizens had joined the pirate fleet.

The camera crews then asked apologetically if they would permit themselves to be broadcast in the act of looting. Growling savagely for their public, and occasionally adding even a fiendish "Ha!" they obliged. The cameramen helped pick out good places to loot for the sake of good pictures. The pirates co-operated in a fine, dramatic style. Millions watching vision sets all over the planet shivered in delicious horror as the pirates went about their nefarious enterprise.

Presently the press of onlookers could not be held back by police. They surrounded the pirates. Some, greatly daring, asked for autographs. Girls watched them with round, frightened, fascinated eyes. Younger men found it vastly thrilling to carry burdens of loot back to the pirate ship for them. Thal complained hoarsely that the ship was getting overloaded. Hoddan ordered greater discrimination, but his pirates by this time were in the position of directors rather than looters themselves. Romantic Waldenian admirers smashed windows and brought them treasure, for the reward of a scowling acceptance.

Hoddan had to call it off. The pirate ship was loaded. It was then the center of an agitated, excited, enthusiastic crowd. He called back his men. One party of three did not return. He took two others and fought his way through the mob. He found the trio backed against a wall while hysterical, adoring girls struggled to seize scraps of their garments for mementos of real, live pirates looting a Waldenian town!

But Hoddan got them back to the ship. He fought a way clear for them to get into the ship. Cheers rose from the onlookers. He got the landing-port shut only by the help of police who kept pirate fans from having their fingers caught in its closing.

Then the piratical spaceyacht rose swiftly toward the stars.

An hour later there was barely any diminution of the excitement inside the ship. Darthian gentleman all, Hoddan's followers still gazed and gloated over the plunder tucked everywhere. It crowded the living-quarters. It threatened to interfere with the astrogation of the ship. Hoddan came out of the control-room and was annoyed.

"Break it up!" he snapped. "Pack that stuff away somewhere! What the hell do you think this is?"

Thal gazed at him dully not quite able to tear his mind and thoughts from this marvelous mass of plunder. Then intelligence came into his eyes. He grinned suddenly. He slapped his thigh.

"Boys!" he gurgled. "He don't know what we got for him!"

One man looked up. Two. They beamed. They got to their feet, dripping jewelry and stray objects of virtu. Thal went ponderously to one stateroom. At the door he turned, expansively.

"She came to the port," he said exuberantly, "and said we were wearin' clothes like they wore on Darth. Did we come from there? I said we did. Then she said did we know somebody named Bron Hoddan on Darth? And I said we did and if she'd step inside the ship she'd meet you. And here she is!"

He unfastened the stateroom door, which had been barred from without. He opened it. He looked in, and grabbed, and pulled at something. Hoddan went sick with apprehension. He groaned as the something inside the stateroom sobbed and yielded.

Thal brought Nedda out into the saloon of the yacht. Her nose and eyes were red from terrified weeping. She gazed about her in purest despairing horror. She did not see Hoddan for a moment. Her eyes were filled with the brawny, piratical figures who were Darthian gentlemen and who grinned at her in what she took for evil gloating.

She wailed.

Hoddan swallowed, with much difficulty, and said quickly: "It's all right, Nedda. It was a mistake. Nothing will happen to you. You're quite safe with me!"

And she was.

# CHAPTER XII

Hoddan stopped off at Krim, by landing-grid, to consult his lawyers. He felt a certain amount of hope of good results from his raid on Walden, but he was desperate about Nedda. Once she was confident of her safety under his protection, she took over the operation of the spaceship. She displayed an overwhelming saccharinity that was appalling. She was sweetness and light among criminals who respectfully did not harm her, and she sweetened and lightened the atmosphere of the spaceyacht until Hoddan's followers were close to mutiny.

"It ain't that I mind her being a nice girl," one of his mustachioed Darthians explained almost tearfully to Hoddan, "but she wants to make a nice girl out of me, too!"

Hoddan, himself, cringed from her society. He would gladly have put her ashore on Krim with ample funds to return to Walden. But she was prettily and reproachfully helpless. If he did put her ashore, she would confide her kidnapping and the lovely behavior of the pirates until nobody could believe in them any more. This would be fatal.

He went to his lawyers, brooding. The news astounded him. The emigrant fleet had appeared over Krim on the way to Walden. Before it appeared, Hoddan's affairs had been prosperous enough. Right after his previous visit, news had come of the daring piratical raid which captured a ship off Walden. This was the liner Hoddan'd brought in to Krim. All merchants and ship owners immediately insured all vessels and goods in space-transit at much higher valuations. The risk insurance stocks bought on Hoddan's account had multiplied in value. Obeying his instructions, his lawyers had sold them out and held a pleasing fortune in trust for Hoddan.

Then came the fleet over Krim, with its letter threatening planetary destruction if resistance was offered to single ships which would land and loot later on. It seemed that all commerce was at the mercy of space-marauders. Risk insurance companies had undertaken to indemnify the owners of ships and freight in emptiness. Now that an unprecedented pirate fleet ranged and doubtless ravaged the skyways, the insurance companies ought to go bankrupt. Owners of stock in them dumped it at any price to get rid of it. In accordance with Hoddan's instructions, though, his lawyers had faithfully, if distastefully bought it up. To use up the funds available, they had to buy up not only all the stock of all the risk insurance companies of Krim, but all stock in all off-planet companies owned by investors on Krim.

Then time passed, and ships in space arrived unmolested in port. Cargoes were delivered intact. Insurers observed that the risk insurance companies had not collapsed and could still pay off if necessary. They continued their insurance. Risk companies appeared financially sound once more. They had more business than ever, and no more claims than usual. Suddenly their stocks went up, or rather, what people were willing to pay for them went up, because Hoddan had forbidden the sale of any stock after the pirate fleet appeared.

Now he asked hopefully if he could reimburse the owners of the ship he'd captured off Walden. He could. Could he pay them even the profit they'd have made between the loss of their ship and the arrival of a replacement? He could. Could he pay off the shippers of Rigellian furs and jewelry from the Cetic stars, and the owners of the bulk melacynth that had brought so good a price on Krim? He could. In fact, he had. The insurance companies he now owned lock, stock, and barrel had already paid the claims on the ship and its cargo, and it would be rather officious to add to that reimbursement.

Hoddan was abruptly appalled. He insisted on a bonus being paid, regardless, which his lawyers had some trouble finding a legal fiction to fit. Then he brooded over his position. He wasn't a businessman. He hadn't expected to make out so well. He'd thought to have to labor for years, perhaps, to make good the injury he'd done the ship owners and merchants in order to help the emigrants from Colin. But it was all done, and here he was with a fortune and the framework of a burgeoning financial empire. He didn't like it.

Gloomily, he explained matters to his attorneys. They pointed out that he had a duty, an obligation, from the nature of his unexpected success. If he let things go, now, the currently thriving business of risk insurance; would return to its former unimportance. His companies—they were his, now—had taken on extra help. More bookkeepers and accountants worked for him this week than last. More mail clerks, secretaries, janitors and scrubwomen. Even more vice-presidents! He would administer a serious blow to the economy of Krim if he caused a slackening of employment by letting his companies go to pot. A slackening of employment would cause a drop in retail trade, an increase in inventories, a depression in industry.

Hoddan thought gloomily of his grandfather. He'd written to the old gentleman and the emigrant fleet would have delivered the letter. He couldn't disappoint his grandfather!

He morbidly accepted his attorney's advice, and they arranged immediately to take over the forty-first as well as the forty-second and -third floors of the building their offices were in. Commerce would march on.

And Hoddan headed for Darth. He had to return his crew, and there was something else. Several something else. He arrived in that solar system and put his yacht in a search orbit, listening for the signal the spaceboat should give for him to come on. He found it. He maneuvered to come alongside, and there was blinding light everywhere. Alarms rang. Lights went out. Instruments registered impossibilities, the rockets fired crazily, and the whole ship reeled. Then a voice roared out of the communicator:

*"Stand and deliver! Surrender and y'll be allowed to go to ground. But if y'even hesitate I'll hull ye and heave ye out to space without a spacesuit!"*

Hoddan winced. Stray sparks had flown about everywhere inside the spaceyacht. A ball-lightning bolt, even of only warning size, makes things uncomfortable when it strikes. Hoddan's fingers tingled as if they'd been asleep. He threw on the transmitter switch and said with Annoyance in his voice:

"Hello, grandfather. This is Bron. Have you been waiting for me long?"

He heard his grandfather swear disgustedly. A few minutes later, a badly battered, blackened, scuffed old spacecraft came rolling up on rocket impulse and stopped with a billowing of rocket fumes. Hoddan threw a switch and used the landing-grid field he'd used on Walden in another fashion. The ships came together with fine precision, lifeboat tube to lifeboat tube. He heard his grandfather swear in amazement.

"That's a little trick I worked out, grandfather," said Hoddan into the transmitter. "Come aboard. I'll pass it on."

His grandfather presently appeared, scowling and suspicious. His eyes shrewdly examined everything, including the loot tucked in every available space. He snorted.

"All honestly come by," said Hoddan morbidly. "It seems I've got a license to steal. I'm not sure what to do with it." His grandfather stared at a placard on the wall. It said archly: *Remember! A Lady is Present!* Nedda had put it up.

"Hmph!" said his grandfather. "What's a woman doing on a pirate ship? That's what your letter talked about!"

"They get on," said Hoddan, wincing, "like mice. You've had mice on a ship, haven't you? Come in the control-room and I'll explain."

He did explain, up to the point where his arrangements to pay back for a ship and cargo turned into a runaway success, and now he was responsible for the employment of innumerable bookkeepers and clerks in the insurance companies he'd come to own. There was also the fact that as the emigrant fleet went on, about fifty more planets would require the attention of pirate ships from time to time, or there would be disillusionment and injury to the economic system.

"Organization," said his grandfather, "does wonders for a tender conscience like you've got. What else?"

Hoddan explained the matter of his Darthian crew and how Don Loris might consider them disgraced because they hadn't cut his throat. Hoddan had to take care of the matter. And there was Nedda... Fani came into the story somehow, too. Hoddan's grandfather grunted, at the end.

"We'll go down and talk to this Don Loris," he said pugnaciously. "I've dealt with his kind before. While we're down, your Cousin Oliver'll take a look at this new grid-field job. We'll put it on my ship. Hm…how about the time down below? Never land long after daybreak. Early in the morning, people ain't at their best."

Hoddan looked at Darth, rotating deliberately below him.

"It's not too late, sir," he said. "Will you follow me down?"

His grandfather nodded briskly, took another comprehensive look at the loot from Walden, and crawled back through the tube to his own ship.

So it was not too long after dawn, in that time zone, when a sentry on the battlements of Don Loris' castle felt a shadow over his head. He jumped a foot and stared upward. Then his hair stood up on end and almost threw his steel helmet off. He stared, unable to move a muscle.

There was a ship above him. It was not a large ship, but he could not judge of such matters. It was not supported by rockets. It should have been falling horribly to smash him under its weight. It wasn't. Instead, it floated down with a very fine precision, like a ship being landed by grid, and settled delicately to the ground some fifty yards from the base of the castle wall.

Immediately thereafter there was a muttering roar. It grew to a howl: a bellow: it became thunder. It increased from that to a noise so stupendous that it ceased altogether to be heard, and was only felt as a deep-toned battering at one's chest. When it ended there was a second ship resting in the middle of a very large scorched place close by the first.

A landing-ramp dropped down from the battered craft. It neatly spanned the scorched and still-smoking patch of soil. A port opened. Men came out, following a jaunty small figure with bushy gray whiskers. They dragged an enigmatic object behind them.

Hoddan came out of the yacht. His grandfather said waspishly:

"This the castle?"

He waved at the massive pile of cut gray stone, with walls twenty feet thick and sixty high.

"Yes, sir," said Hoddan.

"Hm," snorted his grandfather. "Looks flimsy to me!" He waved his hand again. "You remember your cousins."

Familiar, matter-of-fact nods came from the men of the battered ship. Hoddan hadn't seen any of them for years, but they were his kin. They wore commonplace, workaday garments, but carried weapons slung negligently over their shoulders. They dragged the cryptic object behind them without particular formation or apparent discipline, but somehow they looked capable.

Hoddan and his grandfather strolled to the castle gate, their companions a little to their rear. They came to the gate. Nothing happened. Nobody challenged. There was the feel of peevish refusal to associate with persons who landed in spaceships.

"Shall we hail?" asked Hoddan.

"Nah!" snorted his grandfather. "I know his kind! Make him make the advances." He waved to his descendants. "Open it up."

Somebody casually pulled back a cover and reached in and threw switches.

"Found a power broadcast unit," grunted Hoddan's grandfather, "on a ship we took. Hooked it to the ship's space-drive. When y'can't use the space-drive, you still got power. Your cousin, Oliver whipped this thing up."

The enigmatic object made a spiteful noise. The castle gate shuddered and fell halfway from its hinges. The thing made a second noise. Stones splintered and began to collapse. Hoddan admired. Three more unpleasing but not violently loud sounds. Half the wall on either side of the gate was rubble, collapsing partly inside and partly outside the castle's proper boundary.

Figures began to wave hysterically from the battlements. Hoddan's grandfather yawned slightly.

"I always like to talk to people," he observed, "when they're worryin' about what I'm likely to do to them, instead of what maybe they can do to me."

Figures appeared on the ground-level. They'd come out of a sally-port to one side. They were even extravagantly cordial when Hoddan's grandfather admitted that it might be convenient to talk over his business inside the castle, where there would be an easy chair to sit in.

Presently they sat beside the fireplace in the great hall. Don Loris, jittering, shivered next to Hoddan's grandfather. The Lady Fani appeared, icy cold and defiant. She walked with frigid dignity to a place beside her father. Hoddan's grandfather regarded her with a wicked, estimating gaze.

"Not bad!" he said brightly. "Not bad at all!" Then he turned to Hoddan. "Those retainers coming?"

"On the way," said Hoddan. He was not happy. The Lady Fani had passed her eyes over him exactly as if he did not exist.

There was a murmuring noise. A dozen spearmen came marching into the great hall. They carried loot. It dripped on the floor and they blandly ignored such things as stray golden coins rolling off away from them. Stay-at-home inhabitants of the castle gazed at them in joyous wonderment.

Nedda came with them. The Lady Fani made a very slight, almost imperceptible movement. Hoddan said desperately:

"Fani, I know you hate me, though I can't guess why. But here's a thing that had to be taken care of! We made a raid on Walden—that's where the loot came from—and my men kidnapped this girl. Her name is Nedda. Nedda's in an awful fix, Fani! She's alone and friendless, and somebody just has to take care of her! Her father'll come for her eventually, no doubt, but somebody's got to take care of her in the meantime, I can't do it. Hoddan felt hysterical at the bare idea. "I can't!"

The Lady Fani looked at Nedda. And Nedda wore the brave look of a girl so determinedly sweet that nobody could, possibly bear it.

"I'm very sorry," said Nedda bravely, "that I've been the cause of poor Bron's turning pirate and getting into such dreadful trouble. I cry over it every night before I go to sleep. He treated me as if I were his sister, and the other men were so gentle and respectful that I—I think it will break my heart when they are punished. When I think of them being formally and coldly executed..."

"On Darth," said the Lady Fani practically, "we're not very formal about such things. Just cutting somebody's throat is usually enough—but he treated you like a sister, did he? Thal?"

Thal swallowed. He'd been beaming a moment before, with his arms full of silver plate, jewelry, laces, and other bits of booty from the town of Ensfield. But now he said desperately:

"Yes, Lady Fani. But not the way I've treated my sister. My sisters, Lady Fani, bit me when they were little, slapped me when they were bigger, and scorned me when I grew up. I'm fond of 'em! But if one of my sisters'd ever lectured me because I wasn't refined, and shook a finger at me because I wasn't gentlemanly— Lady Fani, I'd've strangled her!"

There was a certain gleam in the Lady Fani's eye as she said warmly to Hoddan:

"Of course I'll take care of the poor thing! I'll let her sleep with my maids and I'm sure one of them can spare clothes for her to wear, and I'll take care of her until a spaceliner comes along and she can be shipped back to her family. And you can come to see her whenever you please, to make sure she's all right!"

Hoddan's eyes tended to grow wild. His grandfather cleared his throat loudly. Hoddan said doggedly:

"You, Fani, asked each of my men if they'd fight for you. They said yes. You sent them to cut my throat. They didn't. But they're not disgraced! I want that clear! They're good men! They're not disgraced for failing to assassinate me!"

"Of course they aren't," conceded the Lady Fani sweetly. "Whoever heard of such a thing?"

Hoddan wiped his forehead. Don Loris opened his mouth fretfully. Hoddan's grandfather forestalled him.

"You've heard about that big pirate fleet that's been floating around these parts? Eh? It's my grandson's. I run a squadron of it for him. Wonderful boy, my grandson! Bloodthirsty crews on those ships, but they love that boy!"

"Very—" Don Loris caught his breath, "very interesting."

"He likes your men," confided Hoddan's grandfather. "Used them twice. Says they make nice, well-behaved pirates. He's going to give them stun-pistols and cannon like the one that smashed your gate. Only men on Darth with guns like that! Seize the spaceport and put in power broadcast, and make sure nobody else gets stun-weapons. Run the country. Your men'll love it. Love that boy, too! Follow him anywhere. Loot."

Don Loris quivered. It was horribly plausible. He'd had the scheme of the only stun-weapon-armed force on Darth, himself. He knew his men tended to revere Hoddan because of the plunder. Don Loris was in a very, very uncomfortable situation. Bored men from the battered spacecraft stood about his great hall. They were unimpressed. He knew that they, at least, were casually sure that they could bring his castle down about his ears in minutes if they chose.

"But…if my men…" Don Loris quavered, "what about me?"

"Minor problem," said Hoddan's grandfather blandly. "The usual thing would be pfft! Cut your throat." He rose. "Decide that later, no doubt. Yes, Bron?"

"I've brought back my men," growled Hoddan, "and Nedda's taken care of. We're through here."

He headed abruptly for the great hall's farthest door. His grandfather followed him briskly, and the negligent, matter-of-fact, armed men who were mostly Hoddan's first and second cousins came after him. Outside the castle, Hoddan said angrily:

"Why did you tell such a preposterous story, grandfather?"

"It's not preposterous," said his grandfather. "Sounds like fun, to me! You're tired now, Bron. Lots of responsibilities and such. Take a rest. You and your cousin Oliver get together and fix those new gadgets on my ship. I'll take the other boys for a run over to this spaceport town. The boys need a run ashore, and there might be some loot. Your grandmother's fond of homespun. I'll try to pick some up for her."

Hoddan shrugged. His grandfather was a law unto himself. Hoddan saw his cousins bringing horses from the castle stables, and a very casual group went riding away as if on a pleasure excursion. As a matter of fact, it was. Thal guided them.

For the rest of that morning and part of the afternoon Hoddan and his cousin Oliver worked at the battered ship's Lawlor drive. Hoddan was pleased with his cousin's respect for his device. He unfeignedly admired the cannon his cousin had designed. Presently they reminisced about their childhood. It was pleasant to renew family ties like this.

The riders came back about sunset. There were extra horses, with loads. There were cheerful shoutings. His grandfather came into Hoddan's ship.

"Brought back some company," he said. "Spaceliner landed while we were there. Friend of yours on it. Congenial fellow, Bron. Thinks well of you, too!"

A large figure followed his grandfather in. A large figure with snow-white hair. The amiable and relaxed Interstellar Ambassador to Walden.

"Hard-gaited horses, Hoddan," he said wryly. "I want a chair and a drink. I traveled a good many light-years to see you, and it wasn't necessary after all. I've been talking to your grandfather."

"Glad to see you, sir," said Hoddan reservedly.

His cousin Oliver brought glasses, and the ambassador buried his nose in his and said in satisfaction:

"A-a-ah! That's good! Capable man, your grandfather. I watched him loot that town. Beautiful professional job! He got some homespun sheets for your grandmother. But about you..."

Hoddan sat down. His grandfather puffed and was silent. His cousins effaced themselves. The ambassador waved a hand.

"I started here," he observed, "because it looked to me like you were running wild. That spacefleet, now... I know something of your ability. I thought you'd contrived some way to fake it. I knew there couldn't be such a fleet. Not really! That was a sound job you did with the emigrants, by the way. Most praiseworthy! And the point was that if you ran hog-wild with a faked fleet, sooner or later the Space Patrol would have to cut you down to size. And you were doing too much good work to be stopped!"

Hoddan blinked.

"Satisfaction," said the ambassador, "is well enough. But satiety is death. Walden was dying on its feet. Nobody could imagine a greater satisfaction than curling up with a good tranquilizer! You've ended that! I left Walden the day after your Ensfield raid. Young men were already trying to grow moustaches. The textile mills were making colored felt for garments. Jewelers were turning out stun-gun pins for ornaments, Darthian knives for brooches, and the song writers had eight new tunes on the air about pirate lovers, pirate queens, and dark ships that roam the lanes of night. Three new vision-play series were to start that same night with space-piracy as their theme, and one of them claimed to be based on your life. Better make them pay for that, Hoddan! In short, Walden had rediscovered the pleasure to be had by taking pains to make a fool of oneself. People who watched that raid on vision screens had thrills they'd never swap for tranquilizers! And the ones who actually mixed in with the pirate raiders—You deserve well of the republic, Hoddan!"

Hoddan said, "Hmm," because there was nothing else to be said.

"Now, your grandfather and I have canvassed the situation thoroughly! This good work must be continued. Diplomatic Service has been worried all along the line. Now we've something to work up. Your grandfather will expand his facilities and snatch ships, land and loot, and keep piracy flying. Your job is to carry on the insurance business. The ships that will be snatched will be your ships, of course. No interference with legitimate commerce. The raids will be paid for by the interplanetary piracy risk insurance companies—you. In time you'll probably have to get writers to do scripts for them, but not right away. You'll continue to get rich, but there's no harm in that so long as you re-introduce romance and adventure to a galaxy headed for decline. Savages will not invent themselves if there are plenty of heroic characters—of your making!—to slap them down!"

"I like working on electronic gadgets," Hoddan said painfully. "My cousin Oliver and I have some things we want to work on together."

His grandfather snorted. One of the cousins came in from outside the yacht. Thal followed him, glowing. He'd reported the looting of the spaceport town, and Don Loris had gone into a tantrum of despair because nobody seemed able to make headway against these strangers. Now he'd turned about and issued a belated invitation to Hoddan and his grandfather and their guest the Interstellar Ambassador—of whom he'd learned from Thal—to dinner at the castle. They could bring their own guards.

Hoddan would have refused, but the ambassador and his grandfather were insistent. Ultimately he found himself seated drearily at a long table in a stone-walled room lighted by very smoky torches. Don Loris, jittering, displayed a sort of professional conversational charm. He was making an urgent effort to overcome the bad effect of past actions by conversational brilliance. The Lady Fani sat quietly. She looked most often at her place. The talk of the oldsters became profound. They talked administration. They talked practical politics. They talked economics.

The Lady Fani looked very bored as the talk went on after the meal was over. Don Loris said brightly, to her:

"My dear, we must be tedious! Young Hoddan looks uninterested, too. Why don't you two walk on the battlements and talk about such things as persons your age find interesting?"

Hoddan rose, gloomily. The Lady Fani, with a sigh of polite resignation, rose to accompany him. The ambassador said suddenly:

"Hoddan! I forgot to tell you! They found out what killed that man outside the power station!" When Hoddan showed no comprehension, the ambassador explained. "The man your friend Derec thought was killed by death rays. It developed that he'd gotten a terrific load on—drunk, you know—and climbed a tree to escape the pink, purple, and green duryas he thought were chasing him to gore him. He climbed too high, a branch broke, and he fell and was killed. I'll take it up with the court when I get back to Walden. No reason to lock you up any more, you know. You might even sell the Power Board on using your receptor, now!"

"Thanks," said Hoddan politely. He added. "Don Loris has that Derec and a cop from Walden here now. Tell them about it and let them go home."

He accompanied the Lady Fani to the battlements. The stars were very bright. They strolled.

"What was that the ambassador told you?" she asked.

He explained without zest.... He added morbidly that it didn't matter. He could go back to Walden now, and if the ambassador was right he could even accomplish things in electronics there. But he wasn't interested. It was odd that he'd once thought such things would make him happy.

"I thought," said the Lady Fani, in gentle melancholy, "that I would be happier with you dead. You had made me very angry. But I found it was not so."

Hoddan fumbled for her meaning. It wasn't quite an apology for trying to get him killed. But at least it was a disclaimer of future intentions in that direction.

"And speaking of happiness," she added in a different tone, "this Nedda…" Bron shuddered, and she said, "I talked to her. Then I sent for Ghek. We're on perfectly good terms again, you know. I introduced him to Nedda. She was vanilla ice cream with meringue and maple syrup on it. He loved it! She gazed at him with pretty sadness and told him how terrible it was of him to kidnap me. He said humbly that he's never had her ennobling influence nor dreamed that she existed. And she loved that! They go together like strawberries and cream! I had to leave, or stop being a lady. I think I made a match."

Then she said quietly:

"But seriously, you ought to be very perfectly happy. You've everything you ever said you wanted, except a delightful girl to marry."

Hoddan squirmed.

"We're old friends," said Fani kindly, "and you did me a great favor once. I'll return it. I'll round up some really delightful girls for you to look over."

"I'm leaving," said Hoddan, alarmed.

"The only thing is, I don't know what type you like. Nedda isn't it."

Hoddan shuddered.

"Nor I, said Fani. "What type would you say I was?"

"Delightful," said Hoddan hoarsely.

The Lady Fani stopped and looked up at him. She said approvingly:

"I hoped that word would occur to you one day. What does a man usually do when he discovers a girl is delightful?"

Hoddan thought it over. He started. He put his hands around her with singularly little skill. He kissed her, at first as if amazed at himself, and then with enthusiasm.

There were scraping sounds on the stone nearby. Footsteps. Don Loris appeared, gazing uncertainly about.

"Fani!" he said plaintively. "Hoddan? Our guests are going to the spaceships. I want to speak privately to Hoddan."

"Yes?" said Hoddan.

"I've been thinking," said Don Loris fretfully. "I've made some mistakes my dear boy, and I've given you excellent reason to dislike me, but at bottom I've always thought a great deal of you. And there seems to be only one way in which I can properly express how much I admire you. How would you like to marry my daughter?"

Hoddan looked down at Fani. She did not try to move away.

"What do you think of the idea, Fani?" he asked. "How about marrying me tomorrow morning?"

"Of course not," said Fani indignantly. "I wouldn't think of such a thing! I couldn't possibly get married before tomorrow afternoon!"